SECRET
STORM

White Dove Romances

9612

SECRET STORM

YVONNE LEHMAN

BETHANY HOUSE PUBLISHERS
MINNEAPOLIS, MINNESOTA 55438

Secret Storm
Copyright © 1996
Yvonne Lehman

Published by Bethany House Publishers
A Ministry of Bethany Fellowship International
11400 Hampshire Avenue South
Minneapolis, Minnesota 55438
www.bethanyhouse.com

Printed in the United States of America by
Bethany Press International,
Minneapolis, Minnesota 55438

Library of Congress Cataloging-in-Publication Data

Lehman, Yvonne.
   Secret storm / Yvonne Lehman.
      p.   cm. — (White dove romances ; 2)
   Summary: High school junior Natalie Ainsworth wants
to get to know Scott Lambert better, but he is afraid of what
she will think if she learns that his mother is an alcoholic.

   [1. Christian life—Fiction. 2. Alcoholism—Fiction.]
I. Title. II. Series: Lehman, Yvonne. White
dove romances ; 2.
PZ7.L5322Se   1996
[Fic]—dc20   95–45107
ISBN 1–55661–706–2   CIP
                                     AC

To
Lori—for her invaluable critiques

David—for police procedure information

Cindy—for medical advice

Crystal—for Zac's name and encouragement

Anne—for editing

Barb and Carol—for their faith in the project

Seven-year-old John for "Justin" inspiration

The righteous cry out, and the LORD hears them;

He delivers them from all their troubles.

The LORD is close to the brokenhearted

And saves those who are crushed in spirit.

—Psalm 34:17–18 (NIV)

YVONNE LEHMAN is the award-winning author of ten published novels, including seven inspirational romances, two contemporary novels, and a biblical novel, *In Shady Groves*. She and her husband, Howard, have four grown children and four grandchildren, and they make their home in the mountains of North Carolina.

One

"Big news, son. Your mother's coming home."

Scott Lambert grimaced, hoping he hadn't really heard what he thought he'd heard. His stomach lurched as if he'd just eaten something rotten.

Swallowing hard on the burning sensation in his throat, his reply came out in a choked whisper that he barely recognized as his own voice. "When?"

"In two weeks."

"No, Dad." He shook his head. "No! Not *now*."

"Look, son," Lawrence Lambert tried to reassure him, "it'll be different this time."

"You've said that before. But it's never different! It's always the same old story!"

"Son . . ." his dad implored helplessly.

Ignoring his father's outstretched hand, Scott pushed past him and through the massive oak doors of the house. He charged down the steps and jumped behind the wheel of his car—a snappy sports model, real cool in a cranberry red that all the girls at Shawnee High said was "to die for." But today he didn't notice the sound of the powerful engine roaring to life at his touch, or feel the buttery leather bucket seats beneath him. All he cared about right now was speed—how fast he could put this latest nightmare behind him.

Tires squealing, he spun out of the drive and took off, barely pausing to turn left at the corner. With no destination in mind, he careened onto the highway and drove like a maniac, praying that highway patrolman Bennigan was still eating his supper at Ruby's Roadside Restaurant.

Two weeks! That's not long enough. I'm just beginning to make friends here. Just getting to know Natalie Ainsworth, the greatest girl in Garden City, Illinois—maybe the greatest girl anywhere.

Scott's classmates claimed he had everything going for him. The car. The big house in the most exclusive section of Garden Acres. The looks—"tall, dark, and handsome," some said. His cousin Cissy often told him he should be a model. She oughta know. She'd done some modeling herself and wanted to be an actress. A few of the other girls at school seemed to like him, too—including Natalie.

Yeah, they *all* thought he had it made. If they only knew!

He hoped they never would.

Realizing that he had driven all the way to Harrisburg, Scott headed for the Garden of the Gods—a local tourist attraction. In happier times, his family had visited Shawnee National Forest on trips to visit his mother's relatives. He'd been intending to check it out again with Natalie now that school had been dismissed for the summer. Well, he needed time to think. Why not now? Why not here?

Scott swung into the parking lot and switched off

the ignition. Although the sun would soon be sinking below the horizon, a few sightseers could still be seen scrambling over the unusual rock formations that contrasted sharply with the more level terrain over which he had been traveling for the past hour. Here, however, the land dipped and swelled like the waves of the ocean—casting purple shadows in the sun's dying rays.

From his vantage point, the sheer cliffs jutted up into the sky like the walls of a great cathedral. There was something reassuring about those massive bluffs—something solid and comforting.

Leaving the car, Scott jogged up a flagstone trail, passing hikers on their way out of the park. Already it seemed that the temperature had dropped several degrees, though he had worked up a sweat—more from his churning emotions, he figured, than from the late afternoon sun filtering through the trees. He didn't stop until he reached the top.

Gulping in deep lungfuls of the brisker air, Scott stepped out onto a sandstone bluff that commanded a breathtaking view of the valley below. As far as the eye could see, the land stretched out in a vast, unspoiled wilderness. Closer by were other bluffs, formed by the melting of a giant glacier that, over time—read the plaque at the base of the mountain—had released tremendous volumes of water, eroding the soft limestone and sandstone rocks.

There was not another person in sight. And when the last car pulled out of the parking lot, Scott was alone. Alone with his thoughts.

He could remember a time when he'd had a real family—himself, his older brother, Zac, his dad . . .

and his mom. In those days, Mom had been about the most important person in his life. She'd baked great chocolate-chip cookies. She'd read his favorite bedtime stories at night and was always around to bandage a skinned knee or settle a squabble with his older brother.

But that was a long time ago.

Then had come all those terrifying, embarrassing episodes that had eventually led to his father's ultimatum: "It's either a clinic or a divorce."

His mother had chosen the clinic—not just once, but time after time. Eventually, unable to cope with her drinking problem, their dad had been forced to make a decision that had blown Scott's mind. He had yanked them away from their neat oceanfront home in Santa Monica, California, and their great friends—and in the middle of Scott's junior year in high school, too! But he really couldn't blame his dad. It was all Mom's fault! They'd moved to Garden City to be near her sister Martha Brysen.

Now it would start all over again . . . in two weeks!

Fists knotted at his sides, Scott shouted at the lonely bluffs, "*Why*, Mom? *Why?*"

The sound returned like a slap in his face. The cliffs flung the words back at him from all directions in cruel mockery. *WHY? . . . momwhy? . . . momwhy? . . . mom why? . . . momwhy? . . . momwhy?* It was an echo of Scott's own questioning heart.

As the sound faded, the last fingers of light disappeared behind a far hill, and a heavy silence—as thick as the darkness—settled over him. A stiff breeze blew his hair into his face. It pushed at his back. It taunted him from the treetops. *It wouldn't take much to step off that boulder. You'd fall for a while and then—splat!—it would be all over.*

He swayed toward the ledge, feeling an urge to jump.

Unnerved by the strong compulsion, Scott shoved his cold, clammy hands into the pockets of his jeans. Fumbling, he felt a small, hard object—the little dove he carried with his loose change. His fingers closed around the object, and he was reminded of the reason he carried it. The dove was a symbol of God's Spirit, always present, never failing. Drawing out the dove, he felt its smooth surface—tiny wings spread in flight—as he backed away from the edge of the great rock.

Scott slumped onto the smooth boulder, forearms braced on his knees, shoulders hunched, head bowed. He remembered the White Dove ceremony at Natalie's church just a few weeks ago, when he'd given his testimony. At that time, he'd felt so confident, so sure that he'd turned all his problems over to God.

I thought I'd unloaded all that junk, Lord. But it's back to haunt me. I'm scared. What if Natalie finds out? She'd never understand something like . . . Mom's problem. I don't want to lose her. But I don't want to lose Mom, either. . . .

With a sob in his throat, he whispered, "There's nowhere else to go, God. I guess I've just got to face whatever comes. I need you, Lord. More than ever."

Scott sniffed and lifted his damp face to the breeze. A crescent moon had risen in the night sky, bathing the wrinkled landscape in a luminous glow. A thousand stars winked reassuringly, as if to remind Scott that he was not alone. God was not asleep.

Slowly, Scott rose. Taking one last look, he turned and, led by the moonlight, made his way down the trail.

———

Scott knew they hadn't heard him come in.

Zac was sitting at the kitchen table, chowing down on a sandwich and a bottle of soda. Their dad was leaning back against the counter top, lines of fatigue etched across his pale forehead. He looked drained, Scott thought. More tired even than during those hectic days and nights when he'd spent countless hours at the hospital helping victims of the tornado that had struck Garden City in the late spring.

"I have to give Helen another chance, Zac," their dad was saying wearily. "She's my wife."

Scott hesitated, then barged on into the kitchen. "Sorry, Dad. I shouldn't have run out the way I did."

The relief at seeing his younger son home safe was evident on Lawrence Lambert's handsome face. But his next words were spoken on a solemn note. "It didn't settle anything though, did it, son?"

Scott shook his head as he headed for the refrigerator, took out a soda, and popped the top. "No, sir. It's like you've always said: We can run, but our problems go with us, or . . ."

". . . are waiting for us when we get back," Zac finished for him, easing some of the tension.

Scott pulled out a chair and gave his older brother a wry grin. It was good to have Zac home for the summer. They hadn't seen much of each other during the school year with Zac finishing his sophomore year at Southern Cal. They had a lot of catching up to do.

Dr. Lambert took a seat across from them and rested his elbows on the table. "Zac and I have been discussing our . . . situation, Scott. I've also spoken with your mother's sister, and we've agreed on a plan that might make things easier. I can take some vacation days, and we'll spend time as a family at the Brysens' lake house on Lake Oakwood."

"You've always loved that place, haven't you, buddy?" Zac asked, giving Scott a playful shove.

"Yeah, it's great." They had stayed at the house many times when visiting Martha and Sheldon Brysen before Uncle Sheldon died. But this would be anything but a casual summer vacation.

Their dad gave them a rundown of the plan. He and their mom would spend a few days alone together before the boys joined them. Then they'd all have time to get reacquainted, slowly, before their mother took over some of the family responsibilities. "I know it's going to be awkward for a while, so . . ."—Lawrence Lambert's expression brightened for the first time— "tell you what we'll do." He pushed away from the table, rocking back in his chair. "You guys can invite a friend to come along with you."

"You think that's wise, Dad? I mean, having other people around . . . right now?"

His dad winced and straightened, plowing his hand through his still-thick hair, only now beginning to silver at the temples. "I don't know, Scott. I know we have to try to help your mother. But at the same time, we have to get on with our own lives, too."

"Mom's going to be fine," Zac insisted, taking a swig of cola. "I dropped in to see her last weekend. She's looking great—better than she has in a long time!"

"That's the spirit, Zac." His dad gave an approving nod. "If we don't believe in her, she'll sense it and may lose her will to try. Martha and Cissy's parents have agreed to do all they can." He sighed heavily. "But I promise you one thing. . . ."

Even Zac lowered his sandwich and stared at his dad. Lawrence Lambert didn't make promises often, and when he did, he kept them.

"This is the *last* time." There was not a sound in the room except for the clinking of the ice maker as it released the frozen cubes—as cold as Scott's heart felt at the moment. "And your mother knows it," he added with an ominous tone of finality.

Scott felt a sick feeling in his gut. He didn't know which would be worse—his mom messing up their lives again, or not having her home again—ever. Weird. A few years ago, he'd thought his parents would always be there for him. Somehow, now, the tables were turned.

———

Scott lay on his back in bed, hands laced behind his neck, staring at the shadows on the high ceiling of his spacious room. The lonely feeling never quite went away—not after Mom had gotten . . . sick, and Zac had left for school. He wondered if his brother was already asleep in his room down the hall.

For a moment, Scott thought of Natalie's small

house—a one story, except for an attic hideaway above the family room that had once been their garage. Now the Ainsworths parked their cars outside in the weather. He smiled, remembering the afternoon of the storm when he and Natalie and her three sisters—mattresses and blankets piled on top of them—had clung to one another, holding hands and praying while a tornado played tag around the neighborhood. Despite some damage to the Ainsworths' living room, God had kept them all safe.

Scott felt suddenly ashamed. He was afraid of losing Natalie when he was just getting to know her, but his dad's loss would be even worse. His father could lose the woman he loved, the woman he'd married, the mother of his children!

Will we ever be a whole family again? Scott puzzled. He knew that a lot of teens looked forward to getting away from their parents, but he was not one of them. After another year, he'd be going away to college. *But I'd sure like to have my mom with me during my senior year at high school.*

He swiped at the wetness on his cheek and turned over, punching the pillow. His dad's words came to mind: *We have to get on with our own lives.*

Scott sighed and closed his eyes. *He's right. I'm going to take him up on his offer. And I know who I'll ask to go to Lake Oakwood with me.*

Two

Natalie heard the *clang, clang, clang* of the stainless-steel spatula banging against the bottom of a pan. With a groan, she rolled over to the edge of the bed and groped for the floor with her bare feet.

The irritating noise meant her dad was home from work. This quarter, Jim Ainsworth was working the night shift at the federal prison where he was a correctional officer. Somehow, despite his long hours, he enjoyed cooking breakfast before he hit the sack, and he didn't like to be kept waiting. He expected his family—wife Jill and all four daughters—to get to the table while everything was still hot.

Natalie had been awake for a while. Old habits, she guessed. School hadn't been out for very long, and she still hadn't gotten used to the idea that she could sleep in for the rest of the summer! Wow!

But how would it feel not to see Scott Lambert every day? The thought was depressing. Still, maybe she'd get to see quite a bit of him, after all.

Just about every young person she knew had pitched in to clean up after the tornado that had touched down twice in Garden City. Now that most of the debris had been carted away, Andy and Stephanie Kelly—the youth directors at church—were calling a special "Mission Break Jam" this morning for anyone between the ages of twelve and nineteen to discuss summer plans for the youth group. That thought—along with the fact that Scott would be at the meeting—propelled Natalie out of bed.

In their telephone conversation last night, he'd mentioned he had something to discuss with her. "Something special," he'd hinted mysteriously. Was he going to ask her for another date?

Natalie jumped into shorts and T-shirt, then hurriedly brushed her shoulder-length brown hair away from her face. "I like your looks," Scott had told her. She smiled at her reflection in the mirror, her deep blue eyes dancing. No need to put on any blush today!

I know I'm not beautiful like my sister Amy . . . or Scott's cousin Cissy. But I really don't care. Who wants to be just another pretty face?

She grabbed her toothbrush and hurried out of her attic bedroom and down the stairs to the hallway, wondering which bath would be free this morning—her sisters' or her parents'?

When she reached the bottom of the stairs, she could hear her mom counting along with the TV aerobics instructor. "Morning, Mom," Natalie called through the doorway.

Jill Ainsworth acknowledged her with a good-morning grunt and continued to jog in place, knees pumping and elbows flapping like a goose ready for flight. Her dark ponytail swished as she turned to smile at her eldest daughter.

Natalie went on to the kitchen. "Morning, Dad."

"Morning, kitten. What'll it be? Waffles? Pancakes? Scrambled eggs? You name it."

"Mmm, waffles. Okay?"

"Sure thing!" He opened the cabinet door to retrieve the mix. "Ruthie coming over?"

"I s'pose." Ruthie Ryan, Natalie's best friend for forever, lived a block and a half away. Early one morning last week, Ruthie had appeared just in time for Jim Ainsworth's famous blueberry pancakes. When he had invited her back "anytime," Ruthie had taken him seriously. She'd been showing up as regular as clockwork every weekday morning since.

"Get your hands washed, honey." Jim poured waffle mix and skim milk into a bowl, then picked up a beater and began to whip the mixture. The waffle iron beeped, signaling that the temperature was right for the first one.

Natalie smiled on the way to her parents' bathroom, seeing that the girls' door was shut. Even at sixteen, her dad still thought of her as a little girl needing to be reminded to wash her hands before meals. She really didn't mind. It sort of made her feel loved and protected.

After her morning ritual, Natalie rushed back up the stairs to her room with her toothbrush. It would be great to have a bathroom of her own. Since her dad worked and slept strange hours, she didn't want to disturb him by keeping her toiletries in her parents' bathroom. And if she left her toothbrush in the girls' bathroom, it would inevitably end up as a scrub brush for someone's tennis shoes!

Hurrying back down again, she had another brilliant idea. If her parents switched bedrooms with her, then her mom wouldn't have to do aerobics in the mornings. She'd get a workout just running up and down those stairs. On second thought, that would never work. Her dad would forever be hitting his head on the slanting walls that formed the inverted "V" of the attic.

Oops! Sorry, God. Didn't mean to complain. I'm just grateful that Dad was able to remodel the attic room for me when rooming with Amy—the bionic cheerleader—got to be a little much!

"Come on in, Ruthie," Natalie heard her mother call from the living room as Ruthie and her little brother, Justin, burst through the front door.

"Where's Pongo?" seven-year-old Justin wanted to know, ignoring Jill's greeting.

"Where are *your* manners? Can't you speak?" Ruthie demanded, her rust-colored curls springing about her face as she shook her finger at her little brother.

The child lifted innocent brown eyes to his sister, identical rusty ringlets bobbing. Kissed by the sun, his face was bright with copper freckles. "Hi, Mrs. Ainsworth and Natalie. *Now* can I see the dog?"

"Out back with Rose." Natalie motioned toward the kitchen door. "She's giving Pongo his breakfast."

Justin raced down the hall, through the kitchen, and out the back door, whistling through his fingers.

"Sorry, guys," Ruthie said with a resigned shrug of her shoulders as she followed Natalie into the kitchen. "I had to bring the 'monster.' Dad goes to work early, and now Mom's decided to take a cosmetology course three mornings a week."

"Then maybe she can tell me what to do with my hair," Jill said, coming through the kitchen door, loose strands straggling out of her ponytail and clinging to her damp forehead. She was breathing hard as she circled the table in a cool-down mode.

Jim smiled at her as if she were the prettiest woman in the world. "I think you're perfect just the way you are."

She walked up to him, snuggling under the arm not occupied with stirring the eggs.

Natalie rolled her eyes. "After all these years, they still act like lovebirds."

"Yuck, Dad, she's sweaty," observed twelve-year-old Sarah, who had dribbled her basketball all the way down the hall and was now sliding into her seat at the table.

"Who cares?" Jim grinned down at his wife, hugging her closer. "When you're as old as we are, you can't see too well. The sense of smell goes, too."

Jill wriggled free of his embrace and punched him—hard—on the arm, to the great delight of the spectators.

"Get the kids in, someone." Jim turned to the stove, stirred the scrambled eggs once more, then scooped them into a bowl.

At that moment, fourteen-year-old Amy appeared in the doorway. "Stand back, everyone, and watch this!"

On that note of warning, she backed up a couple of feet, then ran forward, executing a perfect flip in the air before landing in a Chinese split. "Ta-daah!" She spread her arms dramatically, acknowledging the applause with a regal nod.

"Let me guess," Jim said. "You're a Slinky out of control."

Amy got to her feet in one graceful motion and pushed her blond hair away from her glowing face, then wrinkled her nose affectionately. "Hey, that's a compliment, Dad. You're looking at the future head cheerleader of Shawnee High!"

"You've barely finished your freshman year, Amy," Jill reminded her. "You have a couple of years to wait for all that."

"I know, I know," she moaned. "How I wish time would fly. I just can't wait till cheerleading camp."

"Looked like you were flying pretty high a minute ago." Jim set the bowl of sunny yellow eggs on the table. "When is camp?"

"Two more weeks."

"Two *weeks*!" he scoffed. "The way you're acting, you'd think it was two *years*."

"Well, it seems that long."

"Hold your horses, young lady," Jill admonished her, "and tell Rose and Justin to come in for breakfast."

Amy ran to the back door. "Hey, you two, get in here!" she yelled.

"Says who?" Justin yelled back.

"Says my dad, *that's* who!"

Rose came right away, Justin ambling along behind her.

The Ainsworths spoke in unison, mimicking Jim as

he instructed, "Wash your hands."

"But not in the kitchen sink!" Jill cautioned as the little boy stood on tiptoe to reach the faucet. "The bathroom is in *that* direction."

While the younger ones were washing their hands, Jim put a tall stack of waffles and pancakes on the table, then slipped a pan of golden-brown biscuits out of the oven. He sat down at the head of the table, surveying his handiwork with a sigh of accomplishment.

"Now, who has the verse for the day?" he asked when Rose and Justin returned and took their places.

"I know one!" Justin piped up excitedly.

"You're on, young man."

> "Row, row, row your boat
> Gently down the stream.
> Throw your teacher overboard
> And listen to 'er scream."

"Yikes!" Ruthie shrieked. "I'm so embarrassed!"

Everyone was giggling except Jim, who managed to keep a straight face. "Let's try a Bible verse this time," he suggested patiently.

"Love one another," ten-year-old Rose offered, her cheeks dimpling as she smiled at her dad.

"I think we've had that one before, punkin, but it's a good one." He smiled approvingly at his youngest daughter. "Let's try to remember it during the day. Now, let's pray. Any volun—" He glanced at Justin, who still had an eager look on his face. "Never mind. *I'll* pray."

After the blessing followed by a chorus of "Amens," Jill rose to pour herself a cup of coffee.

Natalie knew she'd eat later, when she'd settled down from her morning workout.

"I just love the way you people do things around here," Ruthie observed. "I'll bet there's not another father in the world who takes orders for breakfast like you, Mr. A."

Jim winked at her over a mouthful of eggs, a pleased expression on his face.

Ruthie sighed. "*My* dad's so grumpy in the morning. And Mom's always off to some meeting or class or something."

"That's why I decided to take *night* classes at the junior college a couple of times a week," Jill said, refilling Jim's mug. "That way I could be home with the family most of the time." She sat back down, stirring in the creamer, creating a miniature whirlpool in her cup. "Being a mom isn't easy, but it's the most important job in the world."

"So don't get married and have children until you're at least thirty-five," Jim quipped, relieving the tension.

"You seem to enjoy it," Ruthie commented, looking from one senior Ainsworth to the other.

Jim was the first to respond. "When you spend every working day around hardened criminals, coming home to this family is a breeze." He glanced at his watch. "Hey, you kids better hurry. Didn't you say Andy's Jam is at eight o'clock?"

With each beat, Natalie's heart began to vibrate like a drum. Hoping no one could hear it, she quickly stabbed her last bite of syrupy waffle. *In just a few minutes, I'll be seeing Scott! Wonder if he'll tell me about that "something special"?*

Three

"Okay, okay, where's the jam? And I hope someone brought bread to go with it!" yelled Stick Gordon as he completed a fancy maneuver with a basketball on his way into the youth room housed in the church basement of the Garden City Community Church.

Several of the guys set up an offensive play, trying to steal the ball from him. But the star of Shawnee High's basketball team was too tall, too good, and too fast for them. He was also the class clown, Natalie thought fondly. She could never be disgusted with the lovable goon for long.

Andy Kelly, the youth director, dismissed Stick's remark with a wave of his hand, while his wife, Stephanie, rolled her eyes.

"That guy's got the IQ of a doorknob," Ruthie mumbled as she and Natalie, along with Amy and Sarah, dodged the rampaging boys and made it to chairs at a long table set up for the meeting.

"Oh, Ruthie, he's only kidding around. You're just mad because, as hard as he tries, Sean can't get the ball away from him."

The pert redhead flashed a wide smile of acknowledgment, her pretty face punctuated with a spattering of freckles.

Ruthie's boyfriend was a hunk, Natalie thought, knowing how her mother detested that term. But no other word would do to describe a guy like Sean Jacson. He'd earned his muscles working out in the school gym. He and Ruthie had been going out together for several months, and Ruthie spoke often about wanting to go steady. Hmm. Might not be a bad idea after all, Natalie decided, thinking of Scott. *She* sure wasn't interested in dating anyone else now that she had a guy in her life— that is, if one date with Scott Lambert counted.

Andy began to rap on the table, shouting above the rumble in the room. "Time to get this show on the road! Take your seats, please."

Sean broke away immediately, seeming relieved to leave the group of would-be basketball greats that were no match for Stick. Sean ran his fingers through his damp, blond hair, beginning to curl on his neck, and slumped into a chair beside Ruthie.

Natalie glanced over her shoulder, looking for Scott. She had hoped to save him a seat next to her. But since this was twelve-year-old Sarah's first time at youth-group meeting, she was sticking close to Natalie. Amy, on the other hand, was one of the most popular girls around and would have plenty of offers from both guys and gals.

"I guess basketball's not my game," Sean grumbled.

Natalie leaned forward to speak past Ruthie. "So what? You were great on the wrestling team last year, Sean."

"Thanks," he said, sitting up a little straighter.

"You always see the best in everyone, don't you, Nat?" Ruthie asked admiringly.

Natalie shrugged. "When it's obvious."

———

I hope that's true, Scott thought, overhearing Ruthie's remark as he came up behind Natalie and spoke to her. *I sure hope she'll see the best in my family, and not the worst.*

"Oh, hi, Scott."

She *seemed* glad to see him, judging from that mega-smile. But before he could say anything more, Andy and Stephanie were calling the group to order. There was no room around the table, so he dragged up a folding chair and sat with some of the other guys behind Natalie and Ruthie.

While the group settled down, Scott studied the back of Natalie's head where her hair fell over her shoulders. A really neat girl. Great personality. Fabulous smile. He'd noticed her on his first day at Shawnee High last January. He'd had one class and study hall with her and had been impressed with her answers in history—which proved she studied—and the fact that she didn't laugh at the crude remarks made by some of the kids—which said plenty about her Christianity. He admired that.

Some of the crowd thought she was a goody-goody. But the storm had proved what kind of stuff Natalie Ainsworth was made of. She was a lot more than a pretty package or a bunch of pious talk. He felt . . . comfortable . . . around her. She didn't act weird, and she wasn't all hung up on the way she looked or what she wore. Not like his cousin, Cissy Stiles—until the day of the tornado, that is. After that, even Cissy thought Natalie was pretty special. In fact, the whole Ainsworth family was special.

His secret smile gave way to a worried frown. Until a few years ago, he'd thought *his* family was perfect. His dad, a respected doctor; his mom, a homemaker who did volunteer work at the hospital; his nineteen-year-old brother Zac. Everything had been great. Just great. Until Mom had ruined everything.

Scott shifted uneasily in his chair. It creaked, bringing a few glances his way. He sat, dead still, until they turned to Andy again. What would Natalie think—if she knew? He gazed longingly at the girl sitting in front of him. *I'd sure like for her to be . . . more than a friend. Maybe—if I'm lucky—she won't have to find out the whole story. . . .*

———

"We called this meeting a Jam because we thought that would bring you all out early in the morning." Andy's good-natured confession snared Natalie's attention.

"What about jelly?" Stick spoke up.

There was a resounding chorus of groans, with a liberal sprinkling of laughter.

Ruthie rolled her big brown eyes. "He'll say *anything* to get attention," she whispered loudly to Natalie.

"Maybe he doesn't get enough at home," Natalie whispered back.

"Jamming means getting down to business, and that's what we need to do right now," Andy said firmly, now that the youth were beginning to listen up.

"First, I want to welcome those of you who are not

a regular part of our youth group," he went on, nodding toward Scott Lambert and several from other churches in town. "But as you know from the mailings and newspaper articles, this is a community effort. Steph will give you a rundown on what we've been doing in our church lately, and why."

"Thanks, Andy." Stephanie smiled at her husband, speaking in a sweet, soft voice that made her sound much younger than her twenty-three years.

The group listened attentively as Stephanie told them about the White Dove program, which included not only a commitment to abstaining from sex before marriage but also showing God's kind of love for the community and the world.

"Andy and I believe the Bible tells us to start right here at home. And that's where *you* come in."

The audience perked up as Stephanie went on to review volunteer efforts after the tornado. Everyone, young and old, had pitched in to clean up the debris that had been scattered over many blocks after several homes had been completely demolished. "Now the needs have changed. Andy?"

He stepped front and center. "We're calling this phase of the project COMMUNITY HELPERS. You don't have to be a part of the White Dove program, though that commitment still stands—especially during summer break with all the temptations that come with greater freedom." He glanced around, making eye contact with those who had signed pledge cards in the spring.

Picking up his notes, he continued. "Now, let's see. We have two categories of work available. There are a few paid positions for some of you who haven't been able to find summer jobs yet—lawn-mowing, house-cleaning, car washing, and a few light construction jobs," he read before looking up. "But there are plenty of volunteer jobs available, too. Some of you are already working in some area—transporting storm victims to rehab, caring for children while their parents get their homes back in order, and so on."

Stephanie began handing out sheets of paper to be passed down the line. "This is an outline of the needs. There's a place to sign your name and the hours you can work. I know most of you will be going on vacation with your families sometime during the summer—some of you right away—so give us those dates, too. If you can only donate a couple of hours a week, we'll take it." She flashed a smile. "And please let your parents know about the project. We need all the help we can get."

After everyone had a sheet, Andy told them to look it over. "You might want to hook up with your friends in work teams. . . ."

"What if you don't have any friends?" Stick interjected with a woebegone expression, his prominent ears and downcast eyes giving him the appearance of a dejected hound.

Colby, a fellow teammate whose handsome brown face lit up with a smile, elbowed him. "Hey, man, what do you think *I* am?"

"Me too! Me too!" This from some of Stick's adoring fans who followed his exploits on the basketball court.

"Oh, I wasn't talking about *myself*. I was referring to some of the *other* guys around here," Stick joked.

With a half turn, Sean looked over his shoulder at the lanky boy who was propping his big feet on the back of Sean's chair. "I'm reconsidering our friendship after the way you hog the ball!"

Stick laughed. "It's all in the way you wear your hair, dude. Yours has got to be juuuuuust right. Like Samson, that other strong guy. Remember him?"

Ruthie poked Sean. "Don't you *dare* cut your curls off." Under her breath, she whispered to Natalie, "If all the guys wore their hair like Stick, you could turn them upside down and get all the painting in Garden City done in a single day!"

Natalie chortled, then covered her mouth with her hand. Stick's hair did resemble a paintbrush on top, cut short above his ears and sticking up like stiff bristles.

"Okay, okay," Andy continued, spreading his hands to squelch the ripple of giggles. "It's up to you. Choose a partner, a team, or work solo. But let's all get involved."

"I choose the prettiest girl in the world," Stick interrupted once more.

All eyes turned toward Amy Ainsworth. Stick made no bones about his feelings for Natalie's younger sister, even though there was not a chance that Amy would give him the time of day even if she were allowed to date— which she wasn't. *House rule: No Ainsworth daughter goes out with a boy until she is sixteen, or is mature enough, whichever comes first*, Natalie recited mentally.

By this time, many of them were hooting like owls, "Who? Who? Who?" As if they didn't know.

"Quit pointing at me!" Amy demanded and turned to her friends with an exasperated sigh, her long blond ponytail swinging around her shoulders.

"Oh, I forgot," Stick persisted. "I have a summer job at the Dairy Bar. But I'm available evenings and Saturdays." He grinned knowingly at Amy.

Quieting the riotous laughter with a firm look, Andy continued, "Some of you will be working in groups of five or six with an adult in charge. If needed, we'll use some of you senior highs to head up some of the groups."

"You'll be on your own for breakfast," Stephanie said in her soft voice, "but we have lots of great cooks who've volunteered to fix lunch. At lunchtime, we'll gather outside for a short devotional when it's clear—inside the church, in case of rain. This is an opportunity to put our Bible study into action and 'let our light shine' for Jesus."

"What if some of the people we ask to help us are not Christians?" asked Billy timidly.

"Good point." Andy nodded. "Part of our objective this summer is to reach people who are not members of any church and who don't know Jesus as their Savior. So be sure to take along a sign-up sheet when you leave."

"And don't limit your search for volunteers to this neighborhood," Stephanie added. "People who never get their hands dirty might like to be included, too."

———

Scott knew exactly what Stephanie meant. It was easier for the "down-and-outers" to come to Jesus because they *knew* they couldn't help themselves, while the affluent were more likely to put their trust in their own resources. *Like some of the people in Garden Acres where I live*, he thought ruefully. *I know several things money can't buy. It can't buy a good family relationship, good friends, health . . . and it sure can't heal a broken heart.*

After prayer, some of the group left to get to work signing up volunteers. Others gathered around to discuss the plan further and decide how to split up into work groups.

Seeing Natalie standing a little to the side, Scott walked over. "Want to go with me to ask my brother to volunteer?"

Natalie felt the sun coming up in her heart. It was probably casting its telltale pink glow on her cheeks, too, from the sudden rush of heat she experienced. She'd already met Scott's dad. Now, she would get to meet his brother. Wasn't it supposed to be a sign a guy really liked you when he took you to meet his family?

"I . . . I'll have to drive Amy and Sarah home first."

"Oh, there's nothing to do there, and Dad's sleeping, so we'd have to be extra quiet," Sarah complained. "Couldn't we just go upstairs to the child center and help Mom and Rose? They were going to show the little kids how to make tray favors for the children's hospital today."

"Sure. I need to see Mom anyway. Be right back, Scott."

———

"What a gorgeous day!" Natalie said after she'd cleared her plans with Scott and was sitting beside him on the front seat of his cranberry sports car. She couldn't believe Mom had let her go. But then both her parents had been impressed with the way Scott had handled things during the tornado that had struck near their house.

"Yeah. Perfect." He wheeled smoothly out of the church parking lot. "Beats those early scorchers we had back in May just before the storm."

Today, Natalie observed, only a few snow-white cumulus clouds drifted in a bright blue late-morning sky. As Scott drove along the neighborhood streets, she rolled down the window to get the full benefit of the fresh breeze. A scent of roses wafted through the car.

"Ah." She breathed in the fragrance. "It's great having the whole summer off. Can you believe that when school begins again, we'll be seniors?"

Scott smiled as he pulled out onto the highway. "Yep. The year we've all been waiting for." He waited while Natalie rolled the window up before he spoke again. "I sort of miss not working in the neighborhood today."

"Me too," Natalie admitted. "But from the looks of this list," she said, glancing down at the papers in her hand, "we're going to be busy all summer."

Looking up, she saw that they were approaching the elegant neighborhood where Scott lived, as well as several other members of his extended family. "Hey, do you suppose your cousin would be interested in helping out?"

Scott was skeptical. "Well, Cissy doesn't get out in the sun much because of her modeling, so she probably couldn't do any outside work. But maybe she could help somewhere else. Wouldn't hurt to ask."

How quickly things changed, Natalie reflected. A couple of months ago, she and Cissy Stiles had never had so much as a single private conversation. The older girl had been much too busy keeping up with all her extracurricular activities—serving as president of the student council, modeling, acting in drama club productions, and running around with the most elite crowd at Shawnee High. Strange, but wonderful, how God had worked through a devastating tornado to bring so many people closer. . . .

These pleasant thoughts were suddenly interrupted by the sharp, staccato tooting of a car horn. Scott shifted to a lower gear and brought the car to a smooth stop in the middle of the road, engine idling. There, backing out of the drive next to Cissy's house, was Katlyn Chander. Scott was laughing as he waited for Katlyn to pull out and move on.

It's not even legal to pull out in front of oncoming traffic . . . much less safe! fumed Natalie to herself as Katlyn waved, sending Scott a dazzling smile.

Spotting Natalie in the passenger's seat, Katlyn's smile froze on her face. Her dark hair brushed her shoulders as she deliberately turned her head away and spun out into the street.

Natalie continued to fret inwardly, then admonished herself. *Watch out, Nat. You're being catty. That's supposed to be Katlyn's specialty.* Besides, she was beginning to realize why she was feeling like a balloon with a slow leak. Katlyn had made it plain several months ago that she liked Scott—and she didn't mean as just a friend. Darting a glance at Scott as he gazed after Katlyn's car, Natalie wondered what he was thinking. Whatever it was, he was still smiling when he turned into the next drive and pulled up to the imposing Georgian mansion where Cissy lived.

"I'll check to see if she's home." He jumped out of the car and sprinted toward the door.

He was back in seconds. "No one here but Cornelia. Let's go."

A few blocks away, Scott drove up a long, curved drive, coming to a stop in front of a two-story brick home, great white columns flanking the front entry. Observing these stately old homes, Natalie got the distinct impression that they were built to last—they'd probably never come down, even under the onslaught of a killer tornado.

"Okay if we go in the back?" Scott asked, interrupting her thoughts.

"Sure." Natalie was pleased. The one other time she'd visited Scott's house—when she'd met his dad—she had been invited in the front door by the housekeeper, a woman who seemed much stiffer than the Stiles' friendly Cornelia. And though Natalie had liked Scott's distinguished-looking father right away, she'd felt a little awed standing in their spacious living room. She'd guessed that her whole house might fit in that one room!

Scott pulled around to the side of the house and parked beside a fire-engine red Camaro.

"Neat car," Natalie observed.

Scott grinned. "Zac's pride and joy. It's a '67."

He took her past geometrically designed shrubbery, neatly trimmed into a hedge that bounded a concrete path leading to a patio out back. There, stretched out on a lounge chair near a fantastic kidney-shaped pool, was a guy who looked like a little older version of Scott. This one was wearing swim trunks, and he was eating a sandwich. On the redwood table nearby was a glass of something cold and sparkling, judging from the ice cubes and the bubbles still rising to the top.

35

"My brother Zac—the lazy one," Scott introduced him.

Zac opened one eye, then squinted up at Scott. Seeing that his brother wasn't alone, he sat up while Scott completed the introductions.

Zac unfolded his tall frame and stood, holding out his hand. "Happy to meet you, Natalie."

His smile produced one deep dimple at the corner of his mouth. Though his dark hair was the color of Scott's, Natalie noticed that Zac's eyes were not the same chocolate brown, but a pale, almost translucent blue—like a freshly washed sky after the rain. Cissy's eyes were that color, Natalie recalled. Good looks sure ran in the family.

Zac knew how to turn on the charm, too, Natalie decided, when he invited her to take a chair, then reached for a shirt and pulled it on, leaving it unbuttoned. "Join me for lunch, you two?"

"Sure. . . ." Scott hesitated, looking to Natalie for confirmation.

She nodded. "Thanks. I'd love to."

Zac lifted his hand. "I'll take care of it." With a jaunty stride, he headed for the back door, called in some instructions, and was back. "Mrs. Krooger will be right out. Now, what brings you to my domain?"

Scott laughed. "*His* domain! *I* live here year-round, *he* comes home from college for the summer and treats *me* like a guest."

"At least he doesn't treat you like an intruder." Natalie liked Scott's brother immediately, enjoying their easy camaraderie. "Where do you go to college?" she asked Zac.

"Southern Cal," he said. "I plan to go to med school."

"Oh. To become a doctor like your dad?"

"I doubt that I'll ever be that good, but a doc, nevertheless. I'm not sure yet what area of medicine. I just know I intend to hang out my shingle someday."

At that moment, the plump Mrs. Krooger wheeled out a cart bearing sandwiches, vegetable sticks, cookies, and punch, then lumbered back into the house.

"Is there any more Coke?" Scott asked, eyeing Zac's glass.

"Believe me, it's not good for you," Zac tossed off his brother's question. "Has pesticides and preservatives and all that bad stuff. Stick with the juice. It's a whole lot healthier."

Natalie sipped her drink. "Delicious!" No doubt it was made from freshly squeezed oranges and lemons. She could see bits of pulp floating in the refreshing beverage. "Beats all those chemicals!"

Zac's dimple flashed. "What did I tell you?"

Soon they were talking like old friends, and before the visit was over, Zac had promised to consider helping out with the community project, though he had offered to recruit a few other guys from the "Club." Natalie assumed he was speaking of the Garden Acres Country Club.

"I like your brother," Natalie said on the drive back home.

Scott looked pleased. "He's a neat guy. I really miss him when he's away at college. We always—well"—he grinned confessionally—"*almost* always—get along great."

Natalie smiled. This had been a special afternoon. She felt that her friendship with Scott had deepened and that she knew him a little better, even if much about him remained a mystery.

When he pulled up in front of her house, he sat at the wheel, as if wanting to say something.

"Wait a minute," he said when she put her hand on the handle of the door. He reached over, flipped open the glove compartment, and retrieved a pair of tickets, which he laid in her lap.

Natalie's eyes widened. "Oh, Scott! Tickets to the Living Waters concert!" She looked at him questioningly. "Where'd you get these? I heard they were sold out weeks ago."

"My dad got them when they first went on sale. Would you like to go with me?"

"Would I ever!"

"Zac gave me his, too, since he already had plans for that night. Anyone you'd like to go along?"

This was incredible. "Ruthie would die if we didn't ask her and Sean! On second thought, she might die if we *do*!"

Scott chuckled, then sobered, holding Natalie's gaze for a heart-stopping moment. "There's another part to the invitation, Nat," he said quietly.

She waited, wondering how Scott could top tickets to the concert. She cocked her head. "What is it?"

"The concert will be held at Lake Oakwood, where my aunt has a summer cottage. Would you . . . stay over with me?"

Natalie gasped, a furious wave of heat rushing to her cheeks. How could she have been so dumb as to think a rich boy like Scott Lambert could possibly be interested in an ordinary person like *her* unless he had something else in mind! What kind of girl did he think she was?

Natalie couldn't get out of Scott's fancy car fast enough! She jerked the door open and swiveled her legs around to the side, ready to bolt.

With a moan of self-disgust, Scott made a grab for her arm. "Please, Nat, don't go! I didn't mean that the way it sounded! Please, let me explain!"

She turned slowly, noting the embarrassed flush that crept all the way to his shirt collar. "Wh-what *did* you mean?"

He shrugged and plunged both hands through his hair. "You must think I'm a jerk. Guess I'm not smooth—like my brother."

He took a deep breath and attempted an explanation, his words tumbling over one another in his haste. "I'm asking you to be our house guest for a few days at my aunt's cottage at Lake Oakwood, that's all, Nat. The whole family will be there—Dad, Zac, me. . . ."

It took a moment for Natalie to piece together what Scott was saying. "Oh, my folks would never let me go somewhere with three guys!" she blurted, then bit her lip, realizing how that must sound to someone like Scott. He would think she was a real prude.

"My . . . mom will be there, too," he added.

Puzzled, Natalie frowned. "But I didn't think she lived with you."

"She's coming home."

Scott's voice had dropped to a hoarse whisper, and he looked terrible. Like he was really miserable about the whole thing. Natalie couldn't help feeling sorry for him.

Then she was shaking her head. "I don't know, Scott. I'd like to go, but I'm not sure." She jumped out of the car and didn't look back. "I'll let you know," she called over her shoulder.

Racing up the walk, Natalie recalled the time Cissy had hinted that Scott was going to ask her to go to the prom with him. He'd told her later—much later—that he'd had to make an unexpected visit to see his mother. But where was the woman? And what was wrong with her? These and other baffling questions swirled about like a miniature tornado in Natalie's head as she hurried into the house.

She paused just inside the door, feeling as if she were caught in a time warp. Everything here looked just as she'd left it this morning—an eternity ago—except this time, Mom was cooking supper, rattling pans in the kitchen. Other familiar sounds intruded into her muddled thoughts. The *thump-thump-thump* of Sarah's basketball on the paved drive at the back of the house, where she shot hoops. Amy's rhythmic chanting as she practiced cheers in her room. Rose's childish squeal as she scuffled with Pongo in the backyard. . . .

How could the rest of the world go on its merry way when her own was topsy-turvy? She felt a fresh stab of regret. She'd probably blown her whole relationship with Scott. After the way she'd treated him in the car, he'd surely ask someone else to go to the concert, not to mention the lakeside vacation. Probably Katlyn Chander! The very idea made Natalie's blood boil. She raced up the stairs to her attic room before anyone spotted her so she could cry in peace.

Four

Natalie floated down the stairs the next morning, her feet barely touching the floor. Funny how one telephone call from Scott the night before could tilt her world right side up again. That—and her parents' decision to let her spend the long Fourth-of-July weekend with Scott's family after the concert.

She barely registered the daily exchange between Justin, Ruthie, and her dad as she drifted into the kitchen, interrupting Justin's latest poetic contribution.

He had screwed up his face as if he'd been struck and was now yelling at Ruthie, "I'm telling!"

"Why? What did I do?" she asked innocently.

> "You kicked me off the bus
> And put ants in my pants;
> Made me do the boogie-dance
> All the way to France."

With that, Justin threw back his head and chortled in a staccato cadence, "Yuk, yuk, yuk."

Ruthie rolled her eyes. "I'm *not* going to let him spoil my week," she declared staunchly. Seeing the

41

dreamy look on Natalie's face, she quizzed, "Who died and left *you* a million bucks?"

"It's better than that, Ruthie. And you're included. . . ."

———————

The rest of the week flew by in a dizzying whirl for Natalie—painting and repairing storm-damaged houses in the Community Helpers program with the youth group during the day and making plans for the big weekend at night. It was decided that Scott would drive the four of them out to the concert on Friday night, rather than go in Sean's old rattletrap. Scott and Natalie would join his family at the lake house afterward, while Sean and Ruthie made the hour-long trip back to Garden City with Andy and Stephanie Kelly, who had been asked to present the White Dove program onstage. She could still hardly believe it!

By Friday afternoon, Natalie had packed and unpacked at least a dozen times. She was waiting when Ruthie arrived, early, to evaluate makeup and hair.

"Can't do anything with this mop of mine," Ruthie moaned. "It's so curly."

"And you're complaining?" Natalie tousled her friend's short curls. "Your hair has never looked better, Ruthie. I love the highlights the sun has given it."

Sitting in front of Natalie's vanity, Ruthie turned her head from side to side. "Yeah, maybe working outdoors all week has paid off."

Natalie had put her own golden-brown hair up on large rollers for added wave and bounce and then had brushed it until it shone. Studying her reflection in the mirror, she was satisfied with the effect. There was just enough curl to flip over her shoulders.

"Don't try to hide your freckles, Ruthie," she scolded. "They're charming."

"*No one* should have *this* much charm," Ruthie griped, making a face at herself in the mirror. But she bypassed the foundation in favor of a light coating of mascara to enhance her brown eyes.

Lightly tanned from their outdoor activity, Natalie needed little more than lip gloss and eye shadow. She loved Ruthie's vibrant appearance, but Natalie preferred a more subdued look for herself.

For the event, they had decided to wear tennis shoes, cutoffs, and their new White Dove T-shirts, the words printed in bold letters on the front, along with the silhouette of a small bird, its wings lifted as if poised for flight. On the back was a Scripture quotation: "The Spirit came down from heaven . . . as a dove" (John 1:32). They would be seeing duplicates of themselves all evening since most of the youth group would be wearing these shirts.

With one last look in the mirror, Natalie and Ruthie raced down the stairs, their glow betraying their heightened sense of anticipation. They breezed into the living room to find Natalie's dad playing checkers with her sister Sarah. The board was set up on the coffee table, Sarah sitting cross-legged on the floor.

Jim looked up over his glasses and gave a low whistle. "Hey, you girls get prettier every day."

"Thanks, Mr. A." Ruthie did a slow turn so he could view her from all angles.

"He's been saying that to me for sixteen years,"

Natalie scoffed. "I must have been some ugly baby." But she cast her father an affectionate look and leaned over to drop a kiss on his forehead. "Dad, shouldn't you still be in bed?" she asked, recalling that he had to leave for work at ten that night.

"Not tonight," he said firmly. "Not until I give that boyfriend of yours my warning look that reminds him he'd better take good care of my little girl."

"Dad, Scott's a Christian, you know."

Jim nodded. "Yes, and so are you. But you're both human, aren't you? No one's immune to temptation. Not even King David, remember? And he was a man after God's own heart."

Ruthie eyed Natalie skeptically. "Does that mean you're going to bathe on a rooftop in your birthday suit like Bathsheba?"

"No, silly—it means I'm going to marry a king!" Natalie retorted.

Their banter was interrupted by Jim Ainworth's disbelieving outburst. "What happened to my checkers when I wasn't looking?"

"I jumped them," Sarah said placidly.

Jim gave her a stern look. "Did you cheat, young lady?"

She giggled. "I don't have to. I'm good at this."

Natalie and Ruthie left the room to make one more assessment of their hair. When they returned to the living room, Scott was already there, talking to Natalie's dad. The flush that warmed Natalie's cheeks was not entirely the result of too much sun.

"I understand your brother may help out with the community youth project," Jim was saying.

Scott shrugged. "Maybe. But only if he can be in charge—even though it's only a squad of lawn mowers this time." Spotting Natalie, he turned to greet her. Just for an instant, the golden glint in his dark eyes reminded her of the way Stick looked at Amy. "Are you ready to go?"

Natalie nodded. "See you guys next week," she said as her family came running in to give her a hug. "It's those two small suitcases, Scott," she directed as he looked around the small entryway for her things.

He bent to retrieve them, and she held the door for him to precede her and Ruthie down the front walk.

"Be sweet," called Jill, her voice slightly tremulous with anxiety.

"Be careful," Jim added, then turned back to his game. "Sarah, you did it again!"

"Great family," Scott commented as they walked toward the car.

"The best," Natalie returned, then amended sensitively, "one of the best, at least." After all, not everyone was as blessed as she. She knew Ruthie's family life wasn't straight out of the script of "Leave it to Beaver." And Scott's? She felt a tingle of anticipation. She'd find out very soon.

———

As soon as Scott pulled up at Sean's white frame house on the edge of town, Sean loped out to meet them.

"Looks like their grass needs cutting," Ruthie pointed out critically before he reached the car.

"So does ours," Natalie reminded her. "We get so

busy helping in the community, we don't have time to take care of our own place."

"I guess he hasn't gotten a White Dove shirt yet."

"Does it matter? Sean always looks great."

Ruthie was beaming. "I couldn't agree with you more!"

Sean's blond curly hair shone golden in the late afternoon sun, and his biceps bulged under the blue knit shirt. But as he approached, he appeared wistful.

"Look, you guys," he said, leaning over to speak to Ruthie through the back window that rolled down smoothly at the touch of a button, "I can't go. You know I applied for the job at the supermarket warehouse. Well, they called a little while ago and wanted me to come in right away so they can show me what I'll be doing. I start tomorrow night."

"On *Saturday*?" Ruthie was incredulous.

"Yeah. Sundays too. They're open seven days a week."

"Oh no!"

"It's not as if I have any choice, Ruthie," he explained apologetically. "I *have* to work. You know how it is. . . ."

"Yeah," she said dejectedly. "I know how it is."

Well, I *don't*, Natalie thought. *Maybe she'll tell me later what this is all about.*

Sean leaned in and kissed Ruthie lightly on the lips. "This means that before long, I can get myself a decent car. Then I can take you out in style."

"I'm riding in style now!" Ruthie shot back, her disappointment edging into bitterness. "I've looked forward to this all week."

"Me too. Really, Ruthie, there's nothing I can do."

"Congratulations on the job, Sean," Scott interrupted, easing the awkward moment.

"Thanks, Scott. Sorry about this." Sean spread his hands helplessly. "I just got the call, so I couldn't let you know sooner."

"No problem, buddy. See ya."

Sean hurried down to his car, a self-proclaimed bomb.

"Well, it's a problem with *me*," Ruthie muttered under her breath. "That's no way for a business to operate . . . call a person at the last minute that way. . . ."

"Maybe they want to see if he's really serious about it," Scott suggested kindly.

"Well, I could tell them what they can do with their job!" Ruthie insisted. "I'd starve to death before I'd work for such an inconsiderate bunch of people!"

Natalie couldn't help but laugh. Her dear friend had a quick temper, but it usually flared and was spent as quickly as a Roman candle on the Fourth of July. "Now, Ruthie. You're proud of Sean for landing a job, and you know it. You're just ticked off because he can't go with us."

"Yes, I am! A chance of a lifetime and now kapooey! And Sean's been telling me the advantages of going steady. Ha!"

"If you don't simmer down, you'll explode," Natalie warned.

Ruthie gave Natalie a sizzling look and leaned over to tap Scott on the shoulder. "Home, James."

"Home? Oh, come on, Ruthie," Natalie said, "you don't have to do that. Why not just go with us?"

"A triangle? No thanks."

"I've got four tickets," Scott went on. "I'd hate to waste two of them."

"Well, I'm not going to be a fifth wheel."

"There are only three of us," Natalie reminded her.

"Same principle."

Natalie glanced at Scott, who rolled his eyes and grinned, then draped his arm over the steering wheel as if preparing to stay for what was shaping up to be a long discussion.

"You're not gonna like this, Ruthie," Natalie began tentatively, "but I have an idea."

"Oh no, not one of *those*!"

"We can still make it a foursome. What about Stick? He never has a date, and I know he'd love to go to the concert."

Ruthie shook her head so vigorously, it appeared as if the red coils of hair would lose their spring. But they continued to bounce saucily around her face as her eyes flashed fire. "You know better, Nat. Besides, he's crazy about Amy."

"Look, it wouldn't be a real date. If you will recall, *I* went to the prom with Stick . . . after waiting for a certain someone to ask me." She slanted Scott a meaningful look. "When he didn't, Stick was the only guy left who didn't already have a date. We went with you and Sean and had a great time. Remember?"

"Yeah, but . . ."

———

Natalie was never quite sure how they managed to talk Ruthie—or Stick, for that matter—into it, but the next thing she knew, they were on their way to Lake Oakwood, the site of the concert featuring one of the hottest stars in contemporary Christian music. Stick had insisted on pedaling his bicycle over to meet them at Natalie's house, so they had doubled back there to pick him up. When he had shown up without a White Dove T-shirt, they'd borrowed one from Sarah, who preferred her shirts large and loose.

Ruthie crawled in back and scooted over to the far side, hugging the door. Stick followed, staying well over on his side and fastening his seat belt, looking as if he were afraid Ruthie might bite.

Scott drove up to the concert site just as the sun was about to set—a blazing ball hanging low in the sky.

"This place is gorgeous!" exclaimed Natalie, taking in the blue-green water, shadowed by the trees fringing the shoreline. Spacious houses—contempory A-lines and older homes, elegant in their many-storied splendor—dotted the banks. Some of the houses clung to the water's edge; others were set far back on sloping green lawns. Here and there, boats shimmied at their docks, ready at a moment's notice for a pleasure cruise or water-skiing.

Ruthie's brown eyes were bigger than usual as she got out of the car and came to stand by Natalie. "So this is how the other half lives?"

Stick merely stared, then shook his bristly head. "Well, let's don't just stand here gawking like a bunch of tourists. We came to hear the music."

Farther down the bank, a floating platform rested on huge pontoons at the edge of the water. On the platform the band was tuning up their instruments: guitars—acoustic and lead; a drum set; some brass, and—in the center of the stage—a synthesizer. Large amplifiers flanked the musicians, ready to blast the airwaves with the latest contemporary Christian sounds.

Here, in this bend of the lake, a hilly bank formed a natural amphitheater. Natalie and Scott glanced over to see several church buses pulling in from towns in the area—their names emblazoned above the front windows: Harrisburg, Carterville, and even as far away as Carbondale. Garden City was conspicuously absent. Natalie knew that with the damage caused by the tornado and the weeks of cleanup, very few young people had thought ahead in time to get tickets for the concert. Probably only a few from home would be here. Well, at least they'd see Andy and Stephanie. Since this concert was a benefit for victims of the tornado, Andy had been asked to explain the White Dove program and how it was being used as a catalyst for all kinds of community service, including the tornado relief.

Seeing their youth leaders, they hurried over to greet them and to find a place to sit as far down front as possible.

"Hope you guys brought a blanket along," Stephanie called cheerfully, "or at least something to sit on. This ground is going to get mighty hard before the night's over!" She made a face and put her hand to the seat of her jeans.

Suddenly, without warning, the varicolored spotlights came on, bathing the platform in shades of hot pink, orange, and green just as the last rays of the sun slid beyond the horizon. As if taking their cue from the spectacular sunset, the group—headed by lead singer

Shane Carter—stepped onto the platform and launched into an up-tempo number that had everyone on their feet, clapping in time to the music. When the last note sounded, echoing across the lake, the applause continued.

"Thanks, guys. Thanks for welcoming Living Waters so warmly. Wow! Lake Oakwood—the perfect setting for our group. Right?" His response was a deafening roar. Shane removed the portable mike from the stand and stepped up toward the front of the stage. "We've been looking forward to this very special weekend ever since we heard about the tornado that had ripped through one of the towns nearby. As you know, one half of the proceeds of this concert will go to aid the homeless and injured in Garden City." This announcement was met by another round of wild applause.

"And to tell you more about what you can do to help, here's your own Andy and Stephanie Kelly from Garden City Community Church!"

Stick whistled between his teeth as Andy and Stephanie moved onto the floating stage and took the microphone, and Ruthie jabbed Natalie with her elbow. "Look! Andy's shaking Shane Carter's hand! If that was me, I'd never wash my hands again!"

In just a few minutes, Andy and Steph had outlined the program and suggested that if anyone needed further information for their own churches back home, brochures would be available out front, along with Living Waters tapes and CDs. "You may notice a few White Dove T-shirts out there tonight, too," Andy went on, gesturing toward the grassy knoll where Scott and Natalie were sitting with Stick and Ruthie. "If you're interested in knowing more about the program or the shirts, just ask. They'll be glad to tell you all about it."

As Andy and Stephanie left the stage, the band began to play, and Shane motioned to the audience to join him in singing an oldie: "There's a sweet, sweet Spirit in this place, and I know that it's the Spirit of the Lord."

Then the group swung into action with a hip-hop beat. And soon Natalie and the others, along with hundreds of other young adults, were standing, lifting their hands toward heaven, and swaying with the music.

One hot tune blended into the next, and the program was drawing to a close before they knew it.

"Before we go, let's join hands and sing a song that Michael W. Smith made famous. I think it sums up what we're feeling here tonight." As the keyboardist struck up the first few chords of "Friends," the crowd jumped to its feet and held hands, forming rows of human chains.

Just as Natalie felt she couldn't hold back the tears another minute, the darkening sky behind the platform suddenly exploded into a burst of blazing color. From a platform far out in the center of the lake, someone was setting off a fireworks display that had been totally unexpected. Bright showers of sparkling color lit the darkness, falling in graceful cascades. Again and again the sharp report could be heard, ricocheting around the lake as the sparklers and Roman candles were launched, sizzling through the sky.

When the fireworks finally died away, Scott was still

holding Natalie's hand. Feeling the joy bubbling up in her, as bright as the diamond dust that had scattered the night, she turned to smile at him. He squeezed her hand in response before they were besieged by a horde of teens and college students, all wanting to ask questions about the White Dove program and how they could start one in their church. At least one or two expressed a desire to become a Christian as a result of the concert.

"Whew!" Ruthie exclaimed when the blitz ended, leaving the four of them to catch their breath. "I'm beginning to appreciate what a celebrity goes through. I thought it was all glamour, but just answering all those questions was really exhausting." She paused, looking around. "There's only one disappointment—I would really have loved to shake Shane Carter's hand," she said dreamily.

"Hey, I'm the one who'd like to shake *your* hand. I believe you guys are the celebrities here tonight."

The four turned in unison, openmouthed, to see Shane Carter and the rest of the band coming up behind them with Andy and Stephanie.

"I've been watching you guys. You did a great job of witnessing out here tonight," Shane complimented them. "That's what these concerts are all about—reaching people for Christ."

When Natalie finally found her voice, she managed to tell the group how fabulous they were and how much she had enjoyed their music. Scott, as usual, said all the right things. But for once, Stick and Ruthie were speechless, gaping at the musicians as if they couldn't believe their eyes.

Shane smiled at Ruthie and took her hand to shake it, her face turning as red as her hair. "My goal is to touch young people with my music and inspire them to reach out to others. Thanks for being a great example."

Stick finally recovered. "He's thanking us! Did you hear that, guys? Mr. Carter's thanking *us*!" he squeaked, his voice cracking as his voice rose.

"Hey," the singer said kindly, "just call me Shane."

When Ruthie and Stick finally joined Andy and Stephanie Kelly for the ride home to Garden City, Ruthie had still not been able to utter a single word.

––––––––––

As Scott and Natalie approached the lake house and turned into the drive, she could barely register much more than a gasp. This was certainly no cottage! It looked more like a mansion to her, set high on a hill. Tall Palladian windows on the front rose two stories, and the entryway overlooking the lake was flanked by a porch on either side. In the front entry, a light had been left on, but apparently Scott's parents were not waiting up for them.

He pulled his little car into the drive at the lake house, rolled down the windows, and switched off the ignition. "Just listen for a minute."

The crickets were tuning up and other night sounds—an owl; the lap of water against the boats, the sound carrying from the shoreline; the soft sighing of the breeze that had blown up—contrasted with the loud blare of music and fireworks earlier in the evening. Natalie had never been so happy in her life. "It's so peaceful here," she sighed, hardly daring to breathe. "Scott, I'll never forget this night as long as I live."

He turned to look at her. "That's sorta what I'd hoped. And just so you don't . . ." He leaned over and brushed her lips in a whisper of a kiss.

Long after Scott had shown her to her room—a guest suite on the second floor—and she had settled in for the night, Natalie lay awake, reliving the moments they had spent together. The concert, the fireworks, the zany antics of their friends, meeting Shane Carter and the Living Waters in person . . . the kiss. . . .

Just as Natalie was drifting off to sleep, a smile on her lips, she heard an unusual sound—almost like a woman crying. She sat up, straining to hear in the darkness, but it didn't come again.

Too tired to hold her eyes open any longer, she closed them, sealing the memories she had stored away in her heart.

Five

Scott sat on the porch that fronted the Brysen lake house, his feet propped up on the railing. Not a soul had been stirring when he'd come out here a few minutes ago, and he was enjoying the chance to sort out his thoughts.

The view was spectacular—the lake mirror clear as far as the eye could see beneath a cloudless azure sky. Great green sentinels—oak, cedar, ash, and pine— guarded the shoreline, where the sun was just breaking free of the eastern horizon.

Man, was he wiped out. He'd been so keyed after the super evening with Natalie that he hadn't slept much. Besides, how could a guy get any rest with a human sawmill sleeping in the same room? Zac had come in really late, fallen across the other twin bed still in his clothes, and started snoring the minute his head touched the pillow.

After that, Scott had heard his mom crying in the master suite across the hall. He wondered what had upset her this time. He sure hoped she didn't plan to hole up in their room the whole time they were here, as she did sometimes when she'd been drinking. On

56

the other hand, he didn't want her to embarrass him in front of Natalie, either. Why couldn't he have had a mom like Jill Ainsworth? Why had he gotten stuck with a woman who was so wrapped up in herself that she didn't even know she had a family?

Well, the mess she had made of things certainly wasn't bothering Zac, Scott thought with a wry grimace. His brother just seemed to let things slide off his back. Maybe life got easier when you were nineteen. . . .

Zac poked his rumpled head out the door and, seeing Scott, shuffled out onto the porch and sat down in one of the cane rockers. "Hey, bro, how was the concert last night? And the little girlfriend?" He slanted Scott a knowing grin.

"The concert was great. Too bad you missed it. And Natalie's just . . . a friend." *Though I'm hoping to change that on this trip*, he thought to himself. "But what about you? Anyone special?"

Zac shook his head. "It's probably a good thing I haven't met anyone special. Getting serious could throw a monkey wrench into my plans for med school. Guess you'll find out soon enough."

Scott was pensive, watching the rosy fingers of dawn creep across the glassy surface of the lake. Overhead, birds called to one another as they dipped and soared. "I don't know if I want to be a doctor."

"*All* the men in our family are doctors, and all the women marry doctors."

It was true. Dad . . . Uncle Sheldon, before he died. Even Cissy Stiles' dad was a hospital administrator. It seemed to be the expected goal of every Lambert male. But Scott wasn't sure he could hack it. "It's a hard life for the family. Look what happened to Mom."

Zac was defensive. "That didn't have anything to do with Dad's being a doctor! She just got . . . sick, that's all. But she's better, or she wouldn't be here."

"Well, *something's* wrong. I heard her crying when we came in last night."

The brothers fell into an uncomfortable silence.

"Have you seen her yet?"

Zac shook his head. "Nope. Dad and Mom were asleep when I got in last night. And when I came down just now, their bedroom door was still shut."

Scott leveled his brother a long look. "And where were *you* 'til two in the morning? It's not like I didn't notice when you came in. We're bunkmates, you know."

"Aw, I was just driving around with some college buddies who were passing through. Didn't think they'd be into a Christian concert."

The toot of a car horn sounded, and Scott looked up to see Aunt Martha's Lincoln driving up.

Cissy hopped out of the front seat, her arms loaded with a stack of magazines. "Hey, you guys, am I glad to see you!" she called. "Just in time to help us unload."

Scott and Zac ran down the steps to the car, relieving Cissy of her magazines and Aunt Martha's cosmetic case. "Looks like our dear aunt has been keeping you locked up. Not a trace of a suntan," Zac observed, accepting Martha's fond kiss on the cheek at the same time she delivered a swat to his backside.

"You know I can't get much sun." Cissy struck a pose with one hand on her hip and the other behind her corn-silk blond head. "It would positively ruin my modeling and acting career," she said in an exaggerated tone.

"Some career," Zac scoffed. "The part of a maid in the senior play."

"Well now, Zac," Aunt Martha put in, stepping onto the porch with a grocery sack, "if she can pull that off, she'll get my vote as a great actress. After all, that girl has never done a lick of work in her life."

"What's all the commotion out here?"

The laughter that had followed Aunt Martha's comment died away as Scott and Zac turned to see their parents stepping out onto the porch, still in their robes. Aunt Martha rushed over to greet them. "How are you, Helen, dear? Lawrence?"

Scott hung back, waiting his turn. It came almost before he was ready. While the others chatted in animated tones, his mother stood behind, in the shadows. She looked really great, he thought with relief, as young and beautiful as ever. Her hair was as blond as Cissy's and her eyes a translucent blue that made her look sort of innocent, like a child. Just looking at her now, nobody would suspect she had a problem in the world. Maybe she really *was* better. . . .

"Scott," she said in that breathy sort of voice he remembered so well. "How wonderful to see you. You . . . you've grown."

It hadn't been *that* long since she'd seen him. He wanted to ask her why she did it—why she kept drinking, why rehab never seemed to work. Didn't her family make her happy? Didn't she love his dad anymore? But of course he couldn't ask those questions. So he copied Zac and did the polite thing. "Hi, Mom," he said, dropping a kiss on her cheek. "How's it going?"

Her reply was too bright, too brittle, almost as

though if she didn't speak quickly, she'd break down and cry. "Oh, I'm just fine, Scott! Really! It's so wonderful here. . . ."

The sound of voices drifted through the upstairs window, waking Natalie with a start. For a moment, she didn't remember where she was. Then . . . Lake Oakwood! Scott! She bolted straight up, tossing her hair out of her face and looking—horrified—at the small clock on the bedside table.

"Oh no! I've overslept! And on my first day here, too! What kind of guest will the Lamberts think I am?"

She brushed her teeth, ran a comb through her hair, and pulled on a fresh T-shirt and shorts. There wouldn't be time for makeup. With a quick glance in the mirror, she took a deep, steadying breath. "Well, this is it, Natalie. You can't keep them waiting all day."

She skimmed the stairs, barely taking in the railed gallery from which the upstairs bedrooms branched off or the massive stone fireplace that rose two stories to a vaulted ceiling. On the front of the house, tall windows afforded a breathtaking view of the lake, shimmering in the sun.

"Nothing like making a grand entrance," she mumbled to herself on the way down, dreading the moment she would encounter the family—the entire family, no doubt, judging from the excited conversation on the porch. She had at least thought Scott would be with her to make it a little easier.

Not giving herself another moment to back out, Natalie stepped through the door. Suddenly, a hush fell over the little group as all heads swiveled to look at her. For a long moment that seemed to stretch from the Fourth of July to Christmas, they stared. Natalie's gaze scanned the faces. Scott's and Zac's were lit up like fireworks. Dr. Lambert's, cautiously cordial. . . . Cissy and Martha Brysen? What were *they* doing here?

Then Natalie's eyes fell on a petite woman standing in the shadow of her tall husband. Short blond curls framed a pretty face, the features finely sculpted like that cameo pin Mom had bought at a garage sale. The pale blue eyes were smudged underneath, with shadows resembling big bruises. And though her lips were tilted upward, the smile appeared to have been painted on—like those of the dolls in Rose's collection.

There was no time for speculation, for just then Cissy stepped forward and smoothly took over. "Nat, you've met Helen Lambert—my Aunt Helen—haven't you? And of course you know Aunt Martha, since she goes to your church. It's great—being here all together like this, isn't it?" Before Natalie could answer, Cissy was grabbing her arm and whisking her inside. "Come on, I'll show you around."

"But I don't understand," Natalie blurted out once they were standing in the great room. "I thought this was a Lambert family vacation."

"It is . . . was. I think at the last minute, Uncle Larry got cold feet—about bringing Aunt Helen here, I mean—and called Martha in as a backup. Actually"—Cissy ducked her head with a grin, her sleek blond hair falling forward—"I tagged along because *my* parents are in Europe, and I didn't want to stay home alone. Besides, Uncle Larry thought *you* might be more comfortable if my cousins and I helped to make up a foursome. Hope you don't mind."

Natalie blinked, taking in all the changes. "Of course I don't mind, Cissy. I'm glad you're here." To her surprise, she found she wasn't just being polite. There were some strange things going on around here, and she'd welcome the company! And ever since the night of the tornado, the elegant, unapproachable Cissy Stiles had become—well, almost a friend. *That storm sure demolished more than houses and trees,* Natalie thought. *It tore down some pretty big barriers between people, too.*

"I'll bet the guys have already had brunch," Cissy was saying. "But Aunt Martha and I just got here, and I'm famished. Let's go see what Rita has for us."

Still practically speechless, Natalie followed her through the great room, past a large, overstuffed recliner and couch, with a pair of loveseats flanking the fireplace. They entered a dining room with a balcony that commanded another view of the lake. "Rita? The cook? They have a cook out here?"

"Sure," Cissy replied breezily. "Rita Dunn lives around here and comes in when the family's visiting. Who wants to cook on vacation?"

The buffet was spread on a long table centered with an airy arrangement of wildflowers. A silver chafing dish—Natalie supposed, since she'd seen them only in pictures—held an assortment of tiny sausage links and crisp bacon; another contained a mound of fluffy, golden eggs. In baskets covered with linen cloths were cinnamon rolls, biscuits, and even bagels with a choice of cream cheese or strawberry preserves. On the sideboard was a pitcher of orange juice and a pot of fresh coffee.

"Wow!" Natalie gasped. "There's enough here for an army."

"Oh, you'd be surprised how fast it will all disappear. The guys will be back for refills, and I don't think everyone has eaten."

They took their plates out onto the balcony—separated from the room by sliding-glass doors—and settled into comfortable deck chairs. At the rear of the house—something Natalie had missed in the dark last night—was an Olympic-sized pool, sparkling in the dazzling sunlight.

Cissy caught her longing glance. "The pool was put in when Uncle Larry decided it was too dangerous to swim in the lake." She nibbled on a piece of bacon. "Hope you won't mind having a roommate while you're here. We'll have to double up, I'm afraid." Cissy gave Natalie a solemn look, her blue eyes as clear as the canopy of sky overhead. "You know, being an only child is not as great as it may sound. I've missed out on a lot. The guys are great fun—but it's not the same as having a . . . sister."

Natalie swallowed a bite and spoke up quickly. "Oh, I don't mind at all—having you as a roommate, I mean. It'll be fun having an *older* sister for a change." She still couldn't believe she was sitting here with *the* Cissy Stiles—the most popular senior at Shawnee High last year.

Cissy seemed pleased. "Ever since the tornado—and what happened with Ron—I've been wanting to get better acquainted with you." She dropped her gaze, the smooth brow puckered in a frown.

"How *is* Ron?"

Before Cissy could answer, Scott and Zac burst through the door, their plates loaded. "Why did you two run off?" Scott demanded. "I wanted Natalie to meet Mom, Cissy."

"I took care of that, didn't I?" She moved her feet out of a chair so he could sit down beside Natalie while Zac dragged up a chaise lounge. "Besides, they'll have plenty of time to get to know each other."

"Not if Mom stays in her room all the time." Scott frowned thoughtfully. "She's gone back to 'rest' now."

"Aw, give her time, bro," Zac chimed in. "She's just tired from her trip."

What trip? Natalie wondered. She really wished she could ask Scott about his mother, but they'd hardly had a minute alone since arriving.

While she and Cissy nibbled on cinnamon buns, the two boys wolfed down their food and chased it with frosty glasses of milk.

"Well, if I'm lucky, that'll last until lunchtime." Zac patted his lean, hard-muscled stomach.

"Forget that, cuz. Rita says she's through for the day. Your dad's grilling steaks tonight." Cissy rose from her chair in one fluid motion. "Right now, we're going swimming."

"Hey!" Scott glared at his cousin. "Natalie's *my* friend. *I* invited her here, so don't go ordering her around."

"Well, excuu-se me." Cissy braced her hands on her hips in that defiant stance Natalie had seen more than once. "So *you* ask her, then."

Scott turned to Natalie with a grin. "Care to go for a swim?"

"I'd love to."

He threw Cissy a smug look. "*That's* how it's done."

Natalie giggled. "And *that*, Cissy, is what it's like having a brother or sister."

"Spare me," Cissy groaned. "Maybe I'm not so deprived, after all. Come on, Natalie. Let's go change—that is, *if* we have Scott's approval."

He motioned them off with a dismissive wave of his hand.

Natalie felt the atmosphere lighten. This was going to be fun. Only people who really liked one another could joke around that way. She and her family did it all the time.

Back in their room, Natalie noticed the huge collection of Barbie dolls lining a bookshelf.

"Those are mine," Cissy explained. "This is the room I've used since I was a little girl. There's another bedroom on the other side of a connecting bath, where my parents usually stay. It's Aunt Martha's this time." She picked up one of the dolls—this one in a red, white, and blue costume. "I've always wished I could look like Barbie."

"Then you've got your wish. They could have used you for the model," Natalie said honestly, rummaging through her suitcase and fishing out her swimsuit.

"I don't mean all over. Couldn't be a model if I were built like her."

Natalie shot her a knowing grin and went into the bathroom to change into her new suit—red with red-and-white straps and a rounded neckline. She quickly fastened her hair back with a ponytail holder.

When she stepped out, Cissy had changed into a

black, form-fitting suit, cut low in front and high on the hips. It was modest enough, though more daring than Natalie's.

"Wow, Cissy! You put even Barbie in the shade!" Natalie eyed herself critically in a full-length mirror. Next to Cissy, she looked almost fat. "I think I should have passed up those cinnamon buns at brunch," she moaned.

"You look great, Nat. Let's go. The guys have probably already hit the pool."

————

Scott and Zac were already in the pool cooling off when the girls came out. Scott sent them a quick glance, while Zac was more openly admiring, complete with whistles.

Remembering their years in California, Scott knew some girls liked to show off their bodies posing around a pool all day in tiny suits. Some of them never even got their suits wet! He had to admit he'd looked. And what he'd seen had been tempting. But looking wasn't a sin. Still, as he'd heard Andy Kelly say, "It's not the birds flying over your head that are a problem; it's only when you let them nest in your hair." Scott was trying to live by that principle—at least, he had ever since he'd signed the pledge to remain sexually pure until marriage. Wincing, he recalled his wilder days. And took comfort in what Andy had said about those who had already blown it. "In Christ," he'd said, "there is forgiveness and a chance to start over."

Scott looked away, giving Natalie time to execute a neat jackknife into the pool without feeling he was staring. She had a nice figure—not as lean and finely contoured as Cissy's, but cute and curvy. He'd better not look too long.

She came out of her dive and cut the water cleanly, swimming with a firm, even stroke to meet him at the edge of the pool.

"Hey, Nat, where did you learn to swim like that?"

She ducked her head into the water and tilted it back, letting the water stream off her face, then laughed at the open look of admiration on his. "Oh, just comes naturally, I guess. Dad says we're all fish in the water."

Then Zac was on the board. He faced forward, leapt off, made a midturn correction, and hit the water—SPLAT!—flat on his stomach, sending a huge surge of water over the sides of the pool.

Scott laughed as the splash rained down on Cissy and Natalie—today was going to be a lot of fun.

———

As the sun angled down toward the horizon and the tangy smell of charcoal and searing steaks filled the air, Scott floated contentedly on his back. While Natalie and Cissy were chatting with Zac near the edge of the pool, Helen Lambert and Aunt Martha were deep in conversation. *What's wrong with this scene?* he thought with a disturbing stab. *It looks so perfect. But looks can be deceiving. I oughta know. I've gotten my hopes up too many times.*

He kept up the charade that all was well as they filled their plates from a table laden with summer bounty grown in Rita Dunn's garden and cooked up ahead of time—golden ears of corn, fresh green beans, fried okra, and plump red tomatoes, picked from the vine that very day. One by one, they found a place to eat—around the umbrella table or on deck chairs pulled up around the pool.

Even while trying to keep up his end of the light conversation over dinner, Scott couldn't quite shake the feeling that something was wrong. He kept darting glances at his mother. She hadn't said much all afternoon—except to Aunt Martha. Fortunately, the others did most of the talking, the topic of discussion one that was very familiar by now—The Tornado. The special counselors at school had said people would be talking about it for years to come.

He was pleased when Natalie fielded questions about her family with ease and grace—questions about her father's work at the federal prison, her mother's classes at the junior college, and each of her three sisters, who were away at camp this week. Natalie sure knew how to fit in, he thought approvingly. She was a good conversationalist, too, her face animated and glowing as she talked. He suspected that even Aunt Martha, who was pretty picky, really liked her. At least, she was listening attentively, her head cocked to one side in that way she had.

Scott didn't relax until after dinner when his dad suggested they take a look at his latest toy—a new Stingray. It was docked lakeside. Leaving Mom and Aunt Martha to put away the leftover food, the four followed his dad down to the edge of the water. But for the life of him, Scott couldn't get his mother off his mind.

———

Zac insisted on taking the boat—a sleek twenty-footer with a black racing stripe painted on the side—out for a trial run. And with an admonition to wear their life preservers and to watch out for some submerged logs on the far side of the lake, Lawrence Lambert waved them off.

Natalie had never had so much fun in her life. She had always loved water sports and was good at them. But she'd never been in a boat—at least, not in a boat like this one! It was the greatest! Skimming the surface of Lake Oakwood; seeing the elegant homes—like dollhouses from this distance; watching the puffs of clouds catch the rosy glow of the fading sunlight; feeling the thrill of being near Scott . . .

They were making their third circuit of the lake at the farthest point opposite the shore—swerving to avoid the logs—when Natalie spotted a small boat bearing down on them. It was traveling at a high speed, carving the water like a knife and sending up a jet spray behind.

At first, it was too far away to make out the person at the wheel. But whoever it was, was fast closing the distance between them. In fact, if someone didn't do something soon, they might be on a collision course! Instinctively, Natalie clung to the side and held on, bracing her feet against the seat in front of her.

When it looked as if they could not avoid impact, Zac swung the Stingray hard to the left, almost tipping it over. "What's the matter with you, you clown?" he yelled, shaking his fist at the slight figure in the white speedboat. "What do ya think you're doing?"

As they passed—only inches apart, it seemed to Natalie—she gazed into a familiar face. Katlyn! Katlyn Chander!

Katlyn waved, tossing her head back, her long, dark hair—like her laughter—trailing in her wake.

Six

Katlyn Chander was still on Natalie's mind the next morning when she awoke in the twin bed next to the window. Cissy had insisted Natalie take that one so she could enjoy the view of the lake first thing. Though it was another picture-perfect day, her thoughts were troubled.

Lord, I'm going to need some help. It's terrific being here—seeing your creative hand in this beautiful place, watching Cissy reach out for you, getting to know Scott's family—to some degree, that is. But what about Katlyn? Please don't let her spoil my time here. . . . Natalie's prayer trailed off when she heard a rustling of sheets as Cissy turned over and cracked one eye.

Seeing that Natalie was awake, she sat up, stretched, and yawned. "Sleep well?" she whispered.

"Like a rock. But why are we whispering? We're both awake."

Cissy crossed her legs on the bed and hugged her pillow as she gestured toward the door. "Aunt Martha. She has eyes in the back of her head, can see through walls, and reads minds."

Natalie nodded. "Now I'm beginning to under-

70

stand. She's part-time chaperone this week, right?"

"In more ways than one," Cissy said mysteriously, assuming a normal tone of voice.

"Let me be sure I've got this straight. She's your *mom's* sister, isn't she?"

"Her older sister—about ten years older. And Scott's mom was born when her parents were middle-aged. I think they call that a 'mistake.'"

Natalie stifled a giggle at the expression on Cissy's face.

"When their parents died, Aunt Martha sort of took over, and she's still doing it." Cissy gave Natalie a knowing look. "You're probably wondering what's going on, aren't you?"

"Well . . . a little."

Cissy shrugged, shifting her pillow. "I'm afraid I can't help you. They won't tell *me* a thing," she said huffily. "My parents said it's family business and if I knew, I'd spill the beans, and before long, it would be all over town." She frowned, then cut her eyes around at Natalie. "They're right, of course. I'd tell you in a heartbeat if I knew."

They laughed together softly. Then Natalie sobered, thinking of the heavy burdens Cissy carried. This girl "who had everything" still didn't get along very well with her parents and had just recently broken up with her boyfriend. And now Scott—Mr. Wonderful himself—was having family problems, too—problems no one cared to discuss. Natalie wouldn't trade places with either of them for all the money in their big, fat checking accounts!

There was a light tap at the door, and Martha

Brysen's voice carried through the paneling. "Are you girls up in there? Wouldn't want you to waste a perfectly marvelous morning!"

———

"Sure, I'll try," Natalie told Scott at breakfast as they sipped orange juice on the balcony outside the dining room and nibbled on freshly baked cinnamon buns, still warm from the oven. "But I warn you, I'm a complete geek when it comes to any sport but swimming."

He grinned at her. "If you're as smart as I think you are, you'll be playing tennis like Steffi Graf in no time."

"Maybe."

"I can play for a while, too," Cissy said, squinting at the cloudless sky, "but I can't risk getting a sunburn. I've got a modeling assignment as soon as we get home. Come on, Zac. Be my partner." She tugged him to his feet.

He agreed, a bit reluctantly, Natalie thought. "Okay. You may have the pleasure of my company 'til evening. That's when I have other plans."

Natalie noticed Scott's dubious look, but when he turned to her, he was all smiles. "Ever played much tennis?"

"Oh, I can hit the ball. It's just that I can't make it go where I want it to go. Dad says I don't know the difference between softball and tennis."

"Maybe we'd better not get too close when she warms up," Zac teased.

After breakfast, the four of them trekked down to the tennis courts about a quarter of a mile from the house. With the holiday weekend in full swing, all but one of the eight clay courts were in use. They hurried to claim the one on the far end.

As they entered, Zac slammed the metal gate behind them, making such a racket that several of the players in the adjoining courts looked up from their play. With an apologetic wave of his hand, Scott suggested they pair off. "Since you're a better player than I am, Zac, you team up with Natalie. I'll take Cissy." Glancing at Natalie, he added, "Let's just hit a few until we get the feel of it."

Throwing Scott a grateful smile, Natalie joined Zac on the opposite side of the net. At least she wouldn't feel quite so pressured to perform.

For a few minutes, they lobbed the ball back and forth, Natalie responding to the challenge. This was fun! And when she made one outstanding return, Zac shouted, "Yes! Who says you're not a tennis player? Now, let's give 'em a run for their money!"

The game was over almost before Natalie got warmed up—due to Zac's superior skill. And the fact that Cissy begged off before they finished playing the entire set left them all dissatisfied.

Zac was plainly disgusted. "Do you have to stop now, Cissy?"

"My face is my fortune, you know." She smiled, revealing perfect, even teeth, the result of a couple of years of braces, she had confessed. "The outdoor look is *out* for this next shoot." With an airy wave of her hand, she jogged over to an umbrella table to sit in the shade, leaving the heavy metal gate ajar.

Zac retreated to a corner to mop his sweaty face

and to take a swig from the bottle of spring water he'd brought with him in his dufflebag.

Obviously impressed with Natalie's performance, Scott motioned her over to his side of the net. "Nat, you've got a great jump smash and forehand. But you could use a few tips on your backhand."

He stood behind her—close—wrapping his hand around hers on the handle of the racket. He guided her arm, pulling it back toward her body, then thrusting it forward in a smooth stroke. For a minute, feeling Scott so near, Natalie lost her concentration. She laughed nervously, hoping he hadn't noticed. Maybe because he really *hadn't* . . . or maybe only because he was such a gentleman, Scott continued to help her with her swing.

"Looking for a fourth?"

Natalie choked. She recognized that voice. She had known—ever since the incident on the lake yesterday—that it was only a matter of time before she'd run into Katlyn Chander again.

Scott turned, Natalie still nestled close to him, before he stepped guiltily away, a slow red flush staining his face. "Well, look who's here! How've you been, Kat?"

It was Katlyn, all right, in a great tennis outfit, its flirty skirt setting off her long, tanned legs. The flowing black hair was pulled back into a loose ponytail, and she was wearing a stylish sweatband across her forehead. She looked—yep, there was no other word for it—*awesome*, to borrow Ruthie's well-worn term.

Once again, glancing down at her own drab shorts and top, Natalie felt a familiar pang. She really didn't fit in here. To make matters worse, Scott—ever the diplomat—was trying to set everyone at ease—and succeeding with only *one* of them!

"Yeah, I lost my partner to the sidelines a minute ago," he said, then added, much too gallantly, Natalie thought, "so why don't you help me save the set? Zac and Nat were giving us a beating."

Katlyn smiled and stepped briskly to the forward spot on the court while Natalie rejoined Zac on the far side. "Their serve, or ours?"

In the next few minutes, she proceeded to show them all that she could do more than look like a picture. To Natalie's dismay, she did it without even breaking a sweat! On the other hand, Natalie was perspiring heavily—as much from nerves, she figured, as from the exercise.

"Wow, Kat!" Scott was apparently dazzled. "Where did you get that serve?"

The dark-haired girl turned a cool glance on Natalie as she replied with a smirk, "From the pro who gave me lessons all winter."

Natalie tried not to feel the stab of hurt that came with her words. She glanced over at Zac. He was taking another long drink from his water container, and when he replaced the cap, she noticed that his hand was trembling. Katlyn and Scott hadn't given him *that* much of a workout. Must be catching a summer virus or something. She watched him lope over to the umbrella table on the other side of the fencing and drop into a chair opposite Cissy.

Right now, Natalie had to be nice to Katlyn, even if it killed her! She just prayed she could mean it.

"Good game, Katlyn." Natalie swiped at a bead of perspiration forming on her upper lip. *Gross! This must look really charming!*

"Thanks." Katlyn swung her racket under one arm and adjusted her sweatband. "And what brings *you* to Lake Oakwood?"

The implication was obvious. Natalie inhaled deeply, wondering if she should count to ten before answering.

But Scott stepped in before she could explain. "*I* did. She's staying with us for a few days."

"I see." Katlyn looked from Natalie to Scott and back again, her frosty smile never reaching the dark brown eyes. She glanced over her shoulder toward Cissy, who was paging through a magazine, an iced drink perched on the table in front of her. "I do recall Cissy saying something about hoping she could find a way to thank you for helping her out during the tornado."

Natalie preferred not to dwell on it, but it suddenly occurred to her that this whole thing might have been set up by Cissy, the Lambert family, and Martha Brysen. They'd been so grateful when Natalie had tried to stop Cissy and Ron from eloping that awful night. Maybe none of it had been Scott's idea at all!

Natalie's thoughts were interrupted by the arrival of an attractive newcomer.

Scott grinned. "Here comes your sister, Kat."

The girl—an older, friendlier version of Katlyn—didn't wait for an introduction, but stuck out her hand. "Hi! I'm Jennifer Chander."

Natalie dried her own sweaty hand on the seat of

her shorts and accepted the warm handshake. "Natalie Ainsworth."

"Welcome to Lake Oakwood. We're having a cook-out tomorrow night at our place. Cissy and Zac have just accepted my invitation. You two tied up?"

"Not really. Sure, we'd love to come," Scott accepted for them, then flashed Natalie an apologetic look. "That is, if Nat wants to."

"Fine." What else could she say?

Natalie thought she heard a low growl coming from Katlyn's direction. She didn't dare look.

"You did okay out there today," Scott told Natalie when Katlyn and Jennifer finally excused themselves to go sailing.

"Well, I sure learned a thing or two." She smiled— a smile of satisfaction. She wasn't quite sure what Scott had in mind. But her dad would have been proud of her. He'd often said that temptation can come quickly and when you least expect it. Katlyn's entrance today had been quite unexpected. Yet, several times on the court, Natalie had resisted the temptation to smash that tennis ball in some most appealing places!

Natalie and Cissy had turned in for the night, after an afternoon of hiking and swimming, when Natalie brought up the subject of Katlyn Chander.

"Oh, she's my next-door neighbor in Garden Acres, you know," Cissy was quick to explain. "Some of our neighbors have summer homes here. The families spend most of the summer on the lake, and the working dads commute or come out on weekends."

Of course. Lake Oakwood was known as a resort for the very rich. That's probably why Garden Acres residents hung out together at school and ignored almost everyone else, Natalie suspected. *But I'm here. And I'm certainly not in their league. But then, who cares? That's not the most important thing,* Natalie thought defensively. *Even Cissy knows it now.*

Deciding not to pursue the subject of Katlyn Chander, Natalie gestured toward a bound volume on the nightstand on Cissy's side. "Is that a script? I thought your parents were dead set against your acting."

Cissy gave a little shrug. "They were opposed to my going to New York or Hollywood and beating on the doors of the studios. They wouldn't finance that, and I had no money of my own—at least, not *that* kind of money. Now I know I was living in a dream world. My only experience was a few high-school plays.

"I guess you could say my folks and I have declared a truce. They've agreed to my getting involved in summer theater—to test how much I really want that kind of career—if I'll go on with my education in the fall."

"Sounds fair to me."

Cissy wrinkled her perfect nose. "It's so weird that just a few weeks ago, I was on my way to marry Ron. I shudder to think that I might have gone through with it. . . ." There was a slight pause. "Can you believe I could now be a married woman—maybe with a baby on the way—and living in a tree house!"

Natalie joined in her soft laughter.

"All it took to change my mind was you, God, and a tornado!"

Later, when the lights were turned out, Natalie lay in bed, looking out at the full moon mirrored in the lake. The Lamberts were really nice people. And she'd even begun to understand and appreciate Martha Brysen a little more. The sometimes-intimidating silver-haired woman had been opposed to the youth group's White Dove movement in the beginning, but she'd changed her mind since then.

Except for Cissy, Natalie wasn't quite sure where she stood with the rest of the family, though. Until today, she'd felt Scott might be beginning to like her as more than a friend. But after the way he'd acted around Katlyn at the tennis courts, she wondered. Had Cissy and her family really engineered the plot to ask her to the lake? And what was going on with Zac? He'd sure been acting strangely all afternoon and evening.

Then there was Scott's mom. Although she always spoke politely at meals and the odd times Natalie had run into her in the house, she didn't know any more about the woman than when she'd first gotten here. In fact, now that she thought of it, Helen Lambert never had much to say to anyone. She just sort of melted into the shadows.

Natalie was startled when Cissy spoke up from the other bed. "Scott thinks your family is the greatest, Nat."

Even in the dark, Natalie could feel a blush coming on at that bit of unexpected acceptance. Then, abruptly, Cissy rolled over and went to sleep, leaving Natalie just as much in the dark as to Scott's true feelings for *her*.

Seven

"If you want to look your best for the party tonight, Nat"—Cissy arched her brow—"I could give you a few tips, if you're interested."

With things winding down for their departure day after tomorrow, the girls were taking a break—for women only, they'd warned Scott and Zac. The guys were off—who knew where—and apparently the senior Lamberts and Aunt Martha were napping.

Natalie shrugged. "Sure, Cissy. I'd be crazy to turn down an offer like that." Natalie was frankly flattered. Not every girl at Shawnee High could take lessons from a real model. Ruthie would be positively green!

"Then let's get started. We've got a lot to do." Cissy bustled into the bathroom and pulled out an assortment of jars and bottles. "Not that you don't already have great-looking skin," she amended hurriedly. "Not even a blemish."

Pinning back Natalie's hair, Cissy instructed her to knot a towel under her arms, leaving her shoulders bare.

Natalie had thought she knew a little about skin care. At least, she'd tried to keep up with some of the teen magazines. But she'd never tried the kaolin-based mask Cissy recommended. And under the older girl's watchful eye, she slathered on a generous scoop of the cream, covering face, neck, and upper chest.

"You'll feel a tingling sensation," Cissy promised, helping her work the cream into her skin.

"*Tingling!* This stuff is opening up my sinuses!" Natalie muttered. She blinked as her eyes teared.

"Oh, come on. Don't wimp out on me. Now that your pores are unclogged, we're ready for Step Two." Cissy snipped off the end of a capsule and stirred it into a moisturizer.

"What's in the capsule?"

"Vitamin E."

"E—isn't that the one that's supposed to make your skin look younger?" When Cissy nodded, still kneading away, Natalie gave her a wry look. "By the time you get through with me, I'm going to be too *young* to go out with Scott!"

Cissy ignored the sassy remark. "And now for the astringent. This contains salicylic acid to get rid of dead cells."

"And all the time, I thought they were alive."

"You're beginning to sound a lot like your friend Ruthie. Now hold still. I'm almost through."

Natalie kept her lips tightly shut as Cissy used cotton balls to swab the delicate areas around eyes, nose, and mouth. She was right. Natalie's skin *did* feel refreshed—almost as well-scrubbed as the time she had "painted" two-year-old Amy with mud after a thundershower. Mom had had to hose off both little girls before giving them a bath!

"There." Cissy stepped back, reminding Natalie of an artist viewing a finished work. "Fantastic! You're beautiful, Nat. I'd better watch out. I may have some competition I hadn't counted on."

Leaning forward, Natalie inspected her reflection in the mirror. She did look pretty good. Of course, the tan helped. She wouldn't have to use any foundation, and since the fresh air and sunshine had brought more color to her face, she could probably even skip the blush. Still, there was Katlyn with her long-lashed dark eyes and lush hair with just the right amount of natural curl. . . .

As if reading her thoughts, Cissy spoke up. "Now for the best part." And before Natalie could move, the girl was closing in on her again, removing the pins and aiming the blow dryer at Natalie's hair, still damp from her shower.

———

By party time, Natalie had—almost literally—been contoured and curried with a fine-tooth comb. Cissy had set Natalie's hair on large rollers for added volume. When it was brushed out, she'd pulled one side back, allowing the other to fall over the face. The ends flipped up in the retro style that was beginning to be popular. And glinting with highlights from the sun, the color was like rich maple syrup.

Since Jennifer had emphasized "ultra-casual," Natalie was wearing her denim shorts and White Dove T-shirt again.

Scott, still sweaty from his afternoon outing, did a double take when he saw her. "Nat? You look incredible!"

Even Zac perked up. "Man, who is *this* babe?"

Natalie laughed good-naturedly along with the guys. But she felt a little prickle of disappointment. So she *was* as ordinary-looking as she'd suspected. If not, the difference wouldn't be so obvious. She shook it off, squaring her shoulders. She'd never minded being ordinary. But Cissy had spent a lot of time and effort in sprucing her up for this party, and she intended to enjoy every minute of it.

When Cissy made her entrance a minute or two later in black capri pants with a midriff-skimming top, the scooped neckline trimmed in yellow daisies, exclamations were in order all over again.

"I don't know about you, Zac, but I think we'd better get cleaned up if we're going to keep up with these two!" Scott joked and took off for their room, Zac right behind him.

On the way they nearly ran over Martha Brysen, who looked rested after her nap. Natalie hadn't yet gotten used to seeing the elegant woman in shorts, although these were cut long—almost to the knee.

"Well, well, if you two don't look spiffy," she complimented them. Natalie supposed the term had been popular in the last century. But Martha was frowning now. "Lawrence and Helen have already left to go into town. They're taking in an art exhibit before joining the Chanders for dinner. I don't like the idea of a party in a home with no adult supervision."

"Oh, Aunt Martha!" Cissy rolled her eyes. "There will be adult supervision. Jennifer's an adult, isn't she? Besides, it isn't as if the rest of us are babies. We know how to handle ourselves. And if we need a reminder, all we have to do is look at Natalie's shirt."

Martha stepped closer to examine the front, then turned Natalie slightly to read the Scripture verse printed on the back. She nodded approvingly. "I must admit, this is a new day—when people actually *wear* their witness."

Actually, Natalie thought, she had worn the shirt not primarily as a way to witness about her faith, but as a reminder to *herself* to live like the Christian she claimed to be. In this unfamiliar environment, it would be easy to drift with the crowd. Sexual purity was one thing, but *living* in purity every day was another. At least three of them—she, Cissy, and Scott—as a result of the White Dove campaign, had pledged to abstain from sexual activity until marriage. With Katlyn around, there was always the chance that Natalie would be tempted to say or do something she'd regret later!

When Scott appeared in an identical shirt, Martha seemed to feel a bit better about the evening. Apparently, though, she couldn't resist one last parting shot. "Now I trust you young people to conduct yourselves properly. Especially you, Zac." She leveled him a stern look. "You're the oldest. The others are only sixteen and seventeen, remember."

Hmph! After all that work to look grown-up, Natalie fumed inwardly, *Martha Brysen can make me feel like a baby!*

"People tell me I look *much* older," Cissy teased. "As a model, I do have an image to keep up, you know."

"You'd do well to remember you're made in the image of God, young lady, and your body is His temple."

"I've been working on my temple all day," Cissy said, giving her aunt a sidelong look, as if wondering if she might be going too far.

"Just make sure you work on your inner temple."

"Now, Aunt Martha," Zac cajoled, walking over to the older woman and placing one arm lightly about her shoulders, "don't you remember how you beautified God's physical temple by donating that gorgeous chandelier to the church? Besides," he lowered his voice and grinned endearingly, "you don't do too badly with your *own* temple. It's obvious where Cissy gets her good looks."

"Oh, get out of here!" the woman said, batting her hand at him fondly. When Zac leaned over to kiss her cheek, Natalie saw that his aunt was actually blushing.

When they piled into Zac's Camaro to drive down to the Chanders', Cissy voiced Natalie's thoughts. "You sure have a way with Aunt Martha, Zac."

"Ah, she's not so tough."

"Well, maybe not . . . at least, not when a guy's as charming as *you*."

Zac smiled in that sort of cocky way he had.

In the cramped backseat, Natalie turned to look over at Scott. Her heart pumped a little faster. He'd changed into his jeans and White Dove shirt. What a thoughtful thing to do. How many guys would be so considerate? On the other hand—and she felt a little ripple of alarm—maybe he'd done it so she wouldn't stick out like a sore thumb among his wealthy neighbors.

She thought again of what Mrs. Brysen had said

about the shirts. Interesting idea: wearing your witness. But to be honest, Natalie thought again, witnessing wasn't her primary objective tonight. No, it was she herself who needed the reminder that she was a Christian. After all, she was going to a party where Katlyn Chander would inevitably be speaking clearly with her well-developed body language—and all for Scott's benefit!

———

The Chander place was one of the contemporary A-frames situated around the lake—not as large or as grand as Martha Brysen's, but very impressive. A two-level deck out back—where the party seemed to be in full swing—jutted up almost to the tall trees. The lower deck seemed to extend beyond the upper one, where there must be a fantastic view.

Jennifer had invited all the young people at the lake—not as many as Natalie had expected. When she saw that most of them were dressed as casually as she and Scott, she began to relax. That is, until she spotted Katlyn, standing in the middle of a group of young people Natalie didn't know. The girl looked smashing in her bright yellow short set, contrasting with her vivid coloring and the olive skin that had deepened to a lovely tan. Natalie couldn't help feeling a tiny bit jealous. How could Scott resist *that* kind of temptation?

"Hey, guys," Jennifer called loudly, motioning them into the great room, which peaked in an inverted V in the center. "Let's be sure we all know each other—at least first names. For you newcomers, we can get better acquainted while we eat. Right now, it's just

Allie"—she winked at a pert blonde with huge cinnamon brown eyes—"Allie's brother, Todd; Jeremiah, Tonya, Cissy, Zac and Scott, and Natalie. Am I leaving anyone out? Oh, and you all know me—the one with the big mouth—and my sister, Katlyn.

"As for food, we opted to keep it simple. We're going to let you do your own thing. The burgers are cooked, and the hot dogs can be microwaved, if you prefer that. All the trimmings—along with chips, dips, and veggie strips—are out on the bar between the rec room and the kitchen. Soda's in the fridge. Help yourself."

What a perfect icebreaker, Natalie thought, grateful for something to do besides stand around and try to make polite conversation with people she didn't know and had nothing in common with. It was even fun bumping into everyone in the kitchen as some nuked the hot dogs and others retrieved icy bottles of Coke and Sprite from the refrigerator.

"Got any milk?" Jeremiah asked, rummaging around.

"Oh no!" Katlyn smacked her forehead with her open palm. "Mom told me to pick up some this afternoon, and I completely forgot. She's gonna *kill* me when there's none for breakfast."

"Don't worry about it, sis. We can get some later at the supermarket in town."

After filling their plates, they drifted out onto the lower deck, finding seats on cedar benches or molded aluminum chairs. Scott sat down beside Natalie, and Katlyn slid over next to him, followed by Jeremiah. When the others returned, conversation came easily.

Jeremiah, a studious-looking boy, would be leaving in a few days for a month's vacation in France—a gift from his grandparents and a reward for graduating as valedictorian of his class. Allie, Jennifer's college roommate last year, would also be a sophomore when they returned to Southern Illinois University in the fall. Allie's brother Todd—who was a masculine version of his sister—would be starting his freshman year there. Tonya—Cissy's age, though not nearly as pretty—had spent last summer in Europe and was full of tips for Jeremiah on how to do France.

Scott confined his remarks to "where I was when The Tornado struck." When he confessed that he had spent the afternoon in Natalie's hallway, wedged under a mattress, there were interested questions from the kids who lived in other towns in the area. Cissy's account of her adventure, told with dramatic suspense, left them breathless.

When it was Natalie's turn, she was more talkative than she'd expected to be. She had them all howling with anecdotes of her family life, especially her sisters—high-energy Amy, ace cheerleader; Sarah, the serious one; and adorable little Rose, the budding artist.

"At the moment, my sisters are all traveling on the Continent—*this* continent," she added, sending them into a fresh outbreak of laughter. Even Katlyn's lips curved in a reluctant smile.

In the lull after the laughter died down, Katlyn spoke. "Charming T-shirt, Natalie. Which boutique carries it?"

Surprised that Katlyn would be so openly sarcastic, Natalie couldn't immediately think how to answer her.

Fortunately, Scott came to the rescue, filling the embarrassing silence. "Same place I got mine. The church would be glad to order one for you."

"I told you about that group at Natalie's church, Kat," Cissy said. "Remember?"

"Oh yeah." Katlyn brushed off the comment and jumped to her feet. "I need a refill."

"Look at that sunset. Spectacular!" Scott pointed toward the blazing ball sliding toward the horizon. "Let's go take a better look upstairs."

Everyone trooped up the outside steps behind him. From that vantage point, Natalie followed his gaze. At the most distant spot—where the lake widened—sky and water met. The blue dome, repeated in the water below, was streaked with pink and orange. And as the fiery rim of the sun struck the surface of the lake, she could almost hear the sizzle.

By the time Katlyn returned, the sunset had faded, and night was coming on. With a toss of her dark head, Katlyn flounced over to Zac, who was leaning back against the railing, his arms folded across his chest. Zac smiled as she approached.

Natalie caught the little scene as it unfolded. *Maybe she isn't flirting*, Natalie told herself, trying to give the other girl the benefit of the doubt. *Maybe standing real close to a guy and looking up into his face is just her way of being friendly*. But Natalie didn't really believe that. At least she could be thankful that Katlyn was staying away from Scott.

Somewhere around the lake a bonfire flared, and sparks—like shooting stars—launched themselves into the darkening sky. The smell of woodsmoke filtered through the air. Natalie tried to take it all in—the sunset, the lakeside bonfire, the rising moon marking a shimmering path across the water, the pungent smoke. She wanted to remember this moment with Scott sitting beside her forever. . . .

But when some of the group went back for refills, another odor drifted to her. From inside, the laughter seemed a little louder than before as it rose to meet her. "Think I'll get a brownie," Natalie told Scott. "Want one?"

When she went downstairs and into the rec room, the odor was stronger. She'd smelled it before at parties where drinking was going on and pairing off soon followed. She'd never stuck around long enough to find out what happened after that.

Through the kitchen door, Natalie could see a dimly lighted room and another bar. Jennifer was pouring something from a bottle into a glass for Allie. *They aren't minors*, Natalie reminded herself, trying not to be judgmental but wondering what she would do if things got out of control.

On the way back to the upper deck, she passed Katlyn coming down for more chips.

"Nice party," Natalie said.

Katlyn shrugged. "Pretty dull, if you ask me."

Natalie sure hoped it would stay that way. At the moment, anyway, no one was being rowdy or loud. Maybe this was just an example of "social drinking"— okay by some people's standards, Natalie knew. At least Cissy, chatting with Todd on the deck below, was empty-handed.

A sudden burst of music startled her. Someone had

put a CD on the player and turned up the sound system. Some rock group, Natalie guessed. It certainly wasn't Shane Carter and the Living Waters!

Jennifer and Allie had still not come back when Zac excused himself and went inside. She hadn't seen Katlyn come out either. Maybe the four of them were talking. Or maybe Zac was just trying to keep Katlyn occupied so she'd leave Scott alone.

Glancing down, Natalie saw Todd put his arm around Cissy. He pulled her closer as he whispered something in her ear.

At that moment Zac and Katlyn emerged from the house—Zac with a glass in his hand. They seemed to be getting along great. Zac lost his balance slightly, grabbing for the railing, and Katlyn giggled.

In fact, apparently everyone had found a partner. Tonya and Jeremiah were deep in conversation on the other side of the deck, Natalie discovered. Maybe she and Scott could finally have some time to talk.

But when she started to suggest it, he appeared upset. He was holding on to the railing so tightly his knuckles were white.

Following his gaze, she saw that he was watching the little scene below. What had upset him? Was it the way Todd had slipped his arm around his cousin? Or was it because Katlyn and Zac were acting so cozy?

"Scott, would you like something else to eat or drink?" Natalie asked, trying to distract him.

It took a moment for her words to sink in. Obviously he was too preoccupied to pay any attention to her, and his face looked positively grim. "Oh, sorry," he said finally, "what did you say?"

She repeated the question.

"No, thanks. I think it's time to leave. Wait here. I'll be right back."

He bounded down the steps to the lower deck and strode over to Zac and Katlyn. Whatever he said wasn't well received. Zac looked disgusted and shook his head. Katlyn put her hand on Zac's arm, as if she were arguing with Scott. Then Katlyn and Zac stalked off and back inside, leaving Scott looking totally dejected.

Natalie turned quickly to Tonya and Jeremiah, interrupting their conversation in French, to tell them goodbye. But she was only trying to cover the sudden ache that gripped her chest. It seemed pretty obvious to Natalie: Scott liked her fine as a friend—but he wanted Katlyn as a girlfriend.

Eight

Scott felt the revulsion well up in him. It was as he'd suspected. Some of the kids in the group were drinking. Beer? Or something stronger? After what had happened with his mom, there was no way *he'd* ever play around with that kind of dynamite. Unfortunately, not everyone felt the way he did.

The college group seemed to be holding it all right, but there were minors present. And he'd been to parties where things got out of hand. He didn't want to hang around waiting to see what would happen, nor did he want anyone he cared for to be mixed up in it.

That's why he was shocked when he walked up to his brother and smelled the booze on his breath. "Come on, Zac," he pleaded, alarmed. "It's time to go."

"I'm not ready to go." Zac was already beginning to look a little glassy-eyed.

Katlyn looped her arm through Zac's and smiled up at him. He returned the smile with that charming, lopsided grin of his.

"Let's go home, then you can do whatever you want," Scott persisted.

"Aw, leave me alone, bro. I'm *doing* what I want."

"Let's go get something else to eat, Zac," Katlyn suggested. "Let *him* take Miss Goody-Goody home. I'll drive you later."

Scott pressed his lips tightly together rather than acknowledge that remark. Sometimes Katlyn could be a real pain. But he was concerned about her. And when she and Zac strode off together across the deck and into the house without a backward glance, Scott didn't know whether to rush after them or let them go.

Zac knows better than this, Scott thought. *He knows what can happen—what our whole family has gone through because of Mom's drinking problem. And Katlyn is only sixteen. . . .*

Shaking his head to clear it, Scott walked over to the corner where Cissy and Todd were acting chummy, Todd's arm still draped around her shoulder. "Excuse me," he broke in, "but I think we'd better leave, Cissy."

"Leave? Scott, it's still early. The night is young." She tilted her head upward to see if he was really serious.

"Some of the crowd has started drinking and . . ."

"Not guilty." She held up her paper cup. "Smell."

"Trust me, Cissy. I know what I'm talking about."

"It's perfectly legit, Scott. They're old enough. Besides, no one's doing anything wrong."

"Really?" He eyed Todd skeptically.

Cissy grinned. "Everything's under control here, cuz."

Todd laughed lightly and lifted his cup in a mock salute.

"Well, I'm worried about Zac. He's had a little too

much, and he's inside with Katlyn."

"So?"

Scott gave Cissy a fierce look. "Come on. I need your help. Maybe *you* can talk some sense into him."

She sighed and rose reluctantly. "Oh, all right. I'll go see what I can do. See ya, Todd."

Inside, Zac and Katlyn were sitting at the bar. Only a faint ray of light from the kitchen filtered into the darkened rec room. It *looked* pretty innocent, but Scott had been to too many parties that had started out that way, only to get real ugly later on. "We're leaving, Zac."

"*Hasta la vista*, little brother."

"Okay. Have it your way. But I think I ought to warn you—I'm planning to call the restaurant and report to Dad just what's going on here."

"You're bluffing."

"No, I'm not. It's not just me. I could walk back. But we have a cousin we're responsible for"—he looked around just in time to see Natalie coming in the door—"and a houseguest, in case you'd forgotten."

Zac slid lazily off the stool, lifted Katlyn's chin with the tip of his index finger and brought her face very close to his. "I'll be back," he whispered. "Don't go 'way."

She nodded. Even in the dim light, her eyes were shining with anticipation. Sensing Scott's stare, she quickly averted her gaze.

After they'd said their goodbyes and had reached the car, Scott asked for Zac's keys.

"No way, little brother. I brought you. And I'm taking you home."

"Let *me* drive, Zac, please," Cissy begged. "I've never driven a terrific car like this."

Zac laughed, a little too loudly. "It's not working, guys. So I had a drink or two. But I know what I'm doing, and no one's driving this baby tonight but *me*." He patted the car affectionately, fumbling with the keys.

"Oh, well, it's not far," Cissy said with a sigh of resignation, sliding into the passenger side while Scott and Natalie climbed in back and belted themselves in.

On the way home, Zac couldn't seem to stop talking. He went on and on about how right Scott was. Kids their age shouldn't be exposed to the evils of alcohol. It spelled nothing but trouble. Didn't he know? Then he changed tactics. "Scott, you shouldn't have said anything in front of—what's her name?—the black-haired babe. Anyway, a little brother shouldn't butt into his older brother's business. Understand, buddy?" When Scott didn't reply, Zac persisted in a sing-song tone. "You're not . . . *answering* . . . me."

"Watch it, Zac!" Cissy said, reaching out for the wheel as Zac turned his head to direct his comment to Scott.

"We can discuss it when we get home," Scott said dully.

At that, Zac gunned the engine, and the little car lurched forward. Fortunately, Scott thought, they didn't have to take any main thoroughfares, and there was no traffic or anyone out for a nightly jog along the side of the road. But Zac almost didn't make the turn onto the long lane leading up to the Brysen house.

After speeding up the drive, Zac slammed on the

brakes, coming to an abrupt stop with a squeal of rubber. He turned off the ignition, hopped out, and attempted to jam the keys in his pocket. Instead, they fell onto the ground.

It was a subdued trio who got out of the car behind him.

"Sorry you had to see that, Natalie," Scott apologized, bending over to pick up the keys.

"Was he upset because you wanted to leave early?"

"That . . . and the fact that he'd been drinking."

Natalie knew this must be hard for Scott. "I was wondering."

"Well, actually, it was a pretty tame party," Cissy put in, "compared to some I've been to."

"Some people just can't handle alcohol, Cissy," Scott said.

Cissy studied her cousin thoughtfully for a long moment, then nodded. "You're right. I have to admit I've tried the stuff, and it tastes awful. Besides, it makes dark circles under my eyes."

Scott grinned affectionately. "And we wouldn't want to do anything to ruin that pretty face, would we?"

By the time they stepped through the doorway leading into the kitchen, Martha Brysen was there to greet them. She looked puzzled. "I didn't expect you back so soon. Anything wrong?"

Cissy spoke for them, her tone casual. "Oh, it was just a get-acquainted time for all the young people around. Nice party."

"Where's Zac?"

"He's gone to his room."

At that moment, there was a thumping sound from the direction of the downstairs bedrooms. "I'll go see what he's up to," Scott said and hurried away, trying to hide his anxiety.

When he reached the room he and Zac were sharing, it was empty. He found Zac in their parents' room across the hall. He was closing the bathroom closet when Scott looked in. "What was the racket?"

"What racket?"

"You know what I'm talking about, Zac."

"Oh, that. It was . . . um, oh yeah, the top of the blanket chest was up. It fell." He shrugged. "So? What's the big deal?"

"I think you'd better go to bed and sleep it off."

"Sure, Papa." Zac's voice dripped with sarcasm. "If *you* say so."

"Sorry. I'm just trying to help." Scott could understand his brother's resentment, but what was he supposed to do? Of all times for their dad to be away. But then, he had his hands full with their mom.

Zac grinned, displaying his old charm. "I know you are, bro. No hard feelings. Go on to your girl. I believe I'll turn in after all."

Scott watched as Zac went into the bathroom and closed the door. He left only when he heard the sound of water running in the sink. Zac must be brushing his teeth before bed.

Scott was carefully noncommittal when he returned to the great room. "Nothing serious. Something fell."

"Well, I'm glad you decided to make it an early night. I think I'll do the same." Mrs. Brysen paused on her way upstairs to her bedroom. "Are you sure Zac's all right?"

Scott laughed uncomfortably. "I think our tennis match this afternoon did him in. He's going to bed."

———

Tennis, Natalie thought. So *that's* where the guys had been all afternoon while she and Cissy were getting ready for the party. Had Katlyn been there, too? Natalie couldn't help but wonder if the dark-haired girl was the cause of the trouble that seemed to be brewing between Zac and Scott. Maybe she'd played up to Zac just to make Scott jealous. Once again, Natalie felt a stirring of uneasiness. If she hadn't been along, maybe none of this would have happened.

"Well, I have a script to study, so I'll say goodnight, too." Cissy blew Natalie and Scott a kiss and skimmed the stairs on her way up to her room.

"Looks like we've been deserted." Scott laughed, a little nervously, when he and Natalie were alone at last. "How about sitting on the patio for a while? We might even catch the late-night cricket concert."

Poor Scott—still trying to make me feel like I'm not an intruder, Natalie thought. But she went along since he seemed to be waiting, holding the sliding door open for her while she went through. She'd excuse herself as soon as possible so he could go back to the party. No doubt Katlyn would be waiting for him.

Lounging on a chaise, Natalie looked up. The moon floated on an ebony sea, studded with stars. Nearby, the branches of a giant oak, drifting in the soft breeze, whispered against the house. It was so romantic. Natalie was sure Scott was wishing he could be sitting here with Katlyn.

Instead, he was slumped in a chair beside her, a slight frown on his face. Natalie could tell he had something on his mind, something he couldn't bring himself to tell her. She'd make it easy for him. She'd say that something had come up at home and she had to get back right away. It wasn't necessarily the Christian thing to do, Natalie thought with wry humor—it was just a matter of self-preservation. Something she had to do for herself before she got any more hung up on Scott Lambert.

She glanced over at him. Before she could open her mouth to speak, he moved closer and took her hand. "Natalie," he began, "I'm glad you decided to come down here with me this week. It's meant a lot. But . . ."

She could fill in the rest. *But it isn't working out the way I expected. You see, I've decided that Katlyn Chander is the girl for me. . . .*

———

Before Scott could continue, the back door slid open and Zac appeared, holding a flashlight. He didn't seem to notice that he was not alone, but moved on toward a small door on the left side of the patio. Zac lifted it and beamed the light under the house, revealing a crawl space containing dirt and pipes.

When Zac dropped down on all fours and crawled in, Scott got to his feet. "I don't believe this," he mumbled and headed over to see what his brother was doing.

Natalie followed close behind.

When they reached him, Zac was clawing around in the dirt. He brushed away a layer of sand, then lifted the top of a wooden crate. Swearing under his breath, he crawled out, empty-handed and covered with dirt.

Scott could smell the booze—stronger, this time. When Zac finally stood to his feet, Scott grabbed his shirt. "Zac! Think what you're doing."

Startled, Zac jerked himself out of Scott's grasp. "Leave me alone. I've got an errand to run."

"You can't go anywhere like this."

"Wanna bet?"

He stumbled away and groped for the car door, bracing himself to keep from falling. He slid under the wheel and felt for the ignition. No keys. "Gimme the keys!" he mouthed at Scott through the window.

Scott shook his head.

Zac threw the door open and got out. "You want to fight me, bro? Is that what you want? In front of this little chick here?"

Scott had never seen his brother so angry. Zac's face was flushed a dark red. "You don't know what you're doing."

"Where've I heard that before?" He choked out a laugh that sounded more like a sob.

Zac frisked Scott, feeling his pockets, then fished for his keys on the left side. Scott tried to hold him off, but his brother's anger gave him added strength, and Zac swung, landing a solid punch.

"Stop it! Oh, please, stop it!" Natalie screamed.

But it was too late. Zac was running for the car again, Scott right behind him.

"Stay here!" Scott yelled at Natalie as he jumped

into the passenger seat, while Zac fumbled to get the key into the ignition.

But he noticed that Natalie had ignored him and was getting into the back. "Let me drive, Zac," Scott said now in a lower tone. "I'll get what you need." He knew exactly what Zac was after. This was not the first time he'd seen someone out of control over booze.

"I'm okay. I know how to drive if I can get this"—he swore softly—"key in here." The engine turned, then sprang to life. He headed the car down the drive. "See?" he said proudly, turning to look at Scott and almost running off the pavement.

"Turn on your lights, Zac!"

"I know, I know," Zac said, irritated, and turned on the light switch, yanking on the steering wheel to correct another miscalculation.

"Watch where you're going!" Scott yelled and grabbed for the wheel. "Fasten your seat belt, Natalie," he called back to her.

"Wipe the ketchup off your face, l'il bro," Zac laughed, slurring his words.

Scott put his hand to his nose. Feeling the wetness, he brought it away and examined his fingers. Blood! In the light from the dash, he could see drops on his shirt, too. It all seemed like a nightmare, or like a horror movie playing out on a screen, except that he had a leading role. Here he was—his brother driving under the influence—an accident waiting to happen—and his mother barely sober from her last stint in rehab. And in the backseat was the finest girl he'd ever met.

What was she thinking? At least now he wouldn't have to tell her anything. She could see the truth about his family with her own eyes. After tonight, she'd never have anything to do with him.

Zac drove slowly, gripping the wheel tightly, as if trying to prove he could stay on the road. But the car began to weave crazily from side to side. Fortunately, Scott thought with a sigh of relief, only one car passed them along the lake road, and the shopping mall was not far.

"The supermarket's right up the street, Zac. Just turn here and pull into a parking place. I'll go in and get the stuff for you."

"Not old enough," Zac mumbled.

"I'll use your ID." Scott was determined to get his brother out from behind that wheel. Once inside the store, he'd call his dad, get him to reason with Zac. But at the same time, Scott knew there would be no reasoning. Maybe he should just call the police. Could he turn his own brother in?

"My ID's not old enough, either." Zac laughed, glancing back at Natalie. "Hear that? My ID's not old enough. What I mean is . . . it's *too* old—it's 'spired."

What! He's driving drunk and with an expired license? Natalie tried to smile, but she was scared to death. Maybe she should jump out of the car while she had time. But that would only upset Zac more. So she kept quiet and prayed.

Scott was still holding on to the wheel, trying to maneuver the car through the crowded parking lot. "Zac, come on. Pull over."

"Leggo. I'll do it," Zac said. "Whoa! Look at that babe. I know *her*."

Natalie looked up. Outside the supermarket were Katlyn and Tonya. Katlyn was carrying a grocery sack; Tonya, a half-gallon jug of milk. Maybe Zac would stop now.

"Hey, baby! You can come to my party *any* day."

Scott was getting angry. "Come on, Zac. Katlyn's only sixteen. She's too young for you."

"Nothing wrong with robbing the cradle once in a while," Zac said drunkenly. He laid on the horn.

Katlyn turned, recognized the car, and waved.

Zac jerked the wheel out of Scott's grasp and aimed for the curb, his speed increasing.

"Brake! Brake!" Scott yelled.

But it was the accelerator pedal Zac pressed.

Natalie watched in horror as Katlyn's eyes widened and her mouth dropped open. Tonya ran to the side; Katlyn appeared frozen, spotlighted like a deer in the headlights. She dropped her bag and pressed her arms against the storefront window, as if trying to melt into it.

Natalie's scream echoed Katlyn's as the car jumped the curb, plowing into the front of the supermarket. Scott was thrown into the windshield, and Natalie lurched forward against the back of the front seat, restrained only by her seat belt.

As soon as the car jolted to a stop, Natalie took in the horrifying scene at a glance. In front of them, the storefront was gone! What had been a massive windowpane was now a gaping hole with huge shards of jagged glass hanging down like stalactites. Some customers, galvanized to action, were milling about. Others, apparently in shock, were rooted to the spot, unable to believe what they were seeing.

Zac was staring uncomprehendingly ahead of him, clutching the steering wheel. But where was Scott?

Natalie quickly unfastened her belt and grabbed the seat in front of her, hoisting herself up. The windshield on the passenger side was smashed. Scott's head and back were scrunched up against the door, his face and hair matted with blood. She could see the white dove on his T-shirt turning crimson before her eyes.

Dazed herself, Natalie shook her head. Everything that had happened so fast now appeared to be unfolding in slow motion. Why was Zac still sitting there? Why didn't Scott move? The low rumble of the gathering crowd intensified to a low roar—or was that the sound of her own heartbeat throbbing in her ears?

Then Natalie spotted Tonya on the fringe of the group pressing around the car. The girl was still holding on to the milk jug, her eyes wide with fright. But where was Katlyn?

I can't just sit here! Natalie jerked open the back door and jumped out. Everyone seemed to be staring at her. Why were they looking at her like that? Why didn't someone do something? Scott needed help.

When she tugged on his door handle, someone shouted, "Don't touch anything!" But the door wouldn't budge. She raced around the back of the car. Zac had managed to open his door and was trying to get out.

By now Scott had pulled himself up, his arms braced against the dashboard and the seat. Blood flowed freely down his face. "I'm okay," he called weakly.

Natalie stepped aside as Zac, holding on to the door, pushed himself out, his back to the accident scene.

The crowd of onlookers had formed a semicircle around the right front fender and were peering down in disbelief. Fearfully, Natalie took a few steps toward the front of the car.

"No! No!" someone screamed. "Oh, please, no." It was only then that Natalie realized the words had come, unbidden, from her own throat. "Someone . . . help her."

A few people glanced toward Natalie, looked disgusted, and turned again to stare at Katlyn, whose legs were pinned between the storefront and the car, her body twisted backward into the store in what seemed an impossible position. She was cut and bleeding, her face and clothing showered with fragments of glass.

Natalie had never seen so much blood in her life. Blood—spurting from a cut on Katlyn's face and dripping down onto the tile flooring. Blood—streaming from Scott's nose, from a gash on his forehead. . . .

Natalie jerked her hand off the car—the blood-red car. She didn't want to look again. Couldn't bear to see. But like the crowd, she couldn't help herself. The hideous scene drew her eyes like a magnet.

She turned again toward Katlyn, the life flowing out of her in a river of red.

Nine

Sirens shrieked through the still night air.

Zac, reeling from the impact and the effects of the alcohol, staggered toward the front of the car and slumped over the hood. "Wha' happened?"

The hum of voices seemed to aggravate him. He lifted his head to find a hostile crowd—some scowling; others advancing toward him menacingly.

"Whatcha think?" he mumbled, his words slurred. "I'm some monkey in a zoo?" He glanced over at the inert form of Katlyn Chander lying on the ground, her body twisted like a discarded doll. "Sh-she was in the way." Peering into the car, he saw Scott, struggling to sit up. "*He* . . . made me do it! He grabbed the wheel!"

Still dazed, Natalie tried to comprehend. But this was more nightmarish than the tornado that had ripped through their town a few weeks ago. Why wouldn't someone do something to help Scott?

A man grabbed her arm roughly. "You kids been drinking?"

Before Natalie could answer, someone in the crowd spoke up. "Well, at least one of them has. The driver's drunk as a skunk."

"Don't worry. He's not going anywhere." A big, burly man approached Zac with fire in his eyes, arms folded across his chest, legs splayed.

Now that they'd started talking, it seemed everyone had something to say. "We've got to move that car off the girl!" called a bystander in an agitated voice. He was immediately challenged by another. "No! We'd better wait for the ambulance. We could do more harm than good." An argument broke out.

"It's too late," a woman rasped during a lull in the debate. "I think she's dead."

The crowd fell silent. Accusing eyes bore into Zac. "I didn't do it . . . I didn't!" he insisted as the reality of what had happened seemed to break through his foggy brain.

Emergency vehicles—an ambulance and a rescue squad—squealed to a stop, their blue-and-red lights flashing.

Zac laid his head down on his arms, sobbing. "I'm sorry. I didn't mean to. Oh, God, let me wake up! Please, let me wake up!"

But the nightmare continued. Natalie tried to take it all in. Scott—pulling himself into a sitting position and wiping the blood from his eyes. Three policemen—getting out of their cruisers, motioning the crowd to stand back. White-coated paramedics—bringing their lifesaving equipment around the front of the car. . . .

Natalie blinked, then watched as the burly guy and one of the police officers wrestled Zac over to a cruiser, where they leaned him over the trunk of the car and patted him down. In the meantime, a couple of emergency technicians pried open Scott's door and helped him out and onto the curb.

"Please." Natalie moved forward. "Let me sit with him." She sank down next to Scott and took his hand. He was still losing a lot of blood. She pulled a tissue from the pocket of her shorts and pressed it against the jagged cut on his forehead.

He winced, but the choking sound he made was not from the pain, Natalie knew, following his gaze as he took in the grisly scene before them. At the front, two more paramedics okayed moving the car off Katlyn's legs as the curious crowd surged forward.

"One minute, she's walking down the street, minding her own business," observed one eyewitness sadly. "The next minute, she's dead!"

"Those three"—another pointed toward Natalie and the two guys—"are responsible. I saw it happen. I think they're drunk."

Having finally freed Katlyn's legs, the paramedics lifted her clear of the wreckage. She was secured by straps to a stretcher, her body still contorted in that weird position.

Scott's grip on Natalie's hand tightened for a moment—then weakened. Feeling him slump against her, she put her arm around him, but he pitched forward onto the pavement.

"Scott! Scott!" He didn't respond. Didn't move. An audible gasp escaped her throat as her gaze fastened on the back of his shirt. She found no comfort, this time, from the words written there: *The Spirit came down from heaven . . . as a dove.*

"Scott!" Seeing his brother's limp body, Zac struggled to reach him but felt his arms pinned firmly behind him.

The technician who was checking Zac for injuries dismissed him with a wave of his hand. "Why is it that it's the drunks who always walk away without a scratch?" he muttered in disgust.

Then someone was forcing Natalie away from Scott, working over him feverishly. One of the EMTs scribbled something on a note pad. "We'd better get this one to the hospital, too."

Natalie staggered to her feet, unable to think clearly. The next thing she knew, someone was taking her pulse and asking her questions. "Are you hurt? Turn your head. Hold out your arms."

But it was Scott who was hurt. Scott, who needed their help. "Let me go with him . . . please." But no one was listening to Natalie. Nor did they pay any attention when she pleaded with them as they lifted Scott onto a stretcher, wheeled him over to a waiting ambulance, and slid the stretcher in beside a white-draped figure. Katlyn!

Natalie was barely able to think. In agonizing fear, she wondered, *Are those Katlyn's feet . . . or is it her head?*

But there was no time to find out. The paramedics jumped inside, slammed the door shut, and fastened it. *Oh God*, Natalie prayed, *they're together. That's what Katlyn wanted. Maybe Scott, too. But not this way. Don't let them be dead. Please, don't let them be dead.*

The driver dashed in behind the wheel, followed by another EMT on the passenger's side. With lights flashing and sirens wailing, they sped out of the parking lot and disappeared into the night.

Natalie stared after the retreating ambulance, tears streaming down her face. Then she looked down at her hands. They were covered with blood—Scott's blood! An awful helplessness stole over her. She didn't know anyone here except Zac, and he was drunk. She couldn't even see Tonya anywhere. Someone must have taken her home.

The crowd was dispersing now—drifting off in pairs or in clusters, still chattering excitedly about the accident. But over their shoulders, they were staring at Natalie as if she were a criminal! As if she had caused this terrible tragedy!

At that moment the policeman who had been interrogating witnesses came over to check on his partner. The second officer had been unsuccessful in getting anything out of Zac, who was blubbering incoherently.

"This one seems okay," one of them observed, gesturing toward Natalie, as if she were not even there. "Just a little shook up. But I think we'd better give her a sobriety test . . . just to make sure."

Turning to her, he looked her straight in the eye. "Say the alphabet."

"S-sir?"

He inhaled deeply, as if bored. "The alphabet, please."

Natalie swallowed hard. Was this some kind of joke? She was no first-grader! But he seemed to be waiting for her answer. "A . . ." she began hesitantly. "B . . ."

"A little faster."

She'd never felt so humiliated. Her lips trembled and her tears started again, but she kept on, pausing only to sniff or hiccup.

He didn't stop her until she got to *M*. "That's enough, young lady. Okay, buddy, your turn," he said, turning to Zac.

Zac looked up, disgruntled. "Wha'?"

"Say your ABCs."

"A . . . B . . . come on, tha's ridi . . ."

"Okay, stand on one leg."

Zac looked around helplessly at Natalie, then glanced over at the pool of blood, where Katlyn had been lying only a short while ago. He grimaced, tried to stand on one leg, lost his balance, and would have toppled over if he hadn't caught himself on the trunk of the cruiser.

The officer unfastened the handcuffs from his belt. "You're under arrest for driving under the influence." He put the cuffs on Zac's wrists. "You have the right to remain silent. Anything you say may be used against you in a court of law. . . ."

"I didn't mean to . . . I wanna see her. Let me tell her . . ."

The cuffs snapped shut. "You have the right to an attorney. . . . If you cannot afford an attorney . . ."

The Miranda Rights completed, the two policemen helped Zac into the backseat and slammed the door.

"I can drive you home, or you can call your parents from the station," the third police officer told Natalie. His tone was coldly impersonal.

"But I don't live here," Natalie said desperately. "I'm visiting with . . . with . . ." She looked around at the people who were leaving the scene, getting into cars to go home to their families. How could she call the lake house and tell the Lamberts that one son was on his way to jail, and the other to the hospital? Scott's parents might not even be home yet, she thought with a sinking sensation, and she'd have to tell Martha Brysen. She just couldn't! "I . . . I don't even know their telephone number." At this last straw, she burst into tears, burying her face in her hands.

"Come on," the officer said, not unkindly, opening the back door of the cruiser. "Let's go."

Frightened, and too stunned to object, Natalie climbed in. A wire cage separated her from the front seat. It seemed unreal, being cooped up like some kind of wild animal.

Although no one had directly said to her, "You have the right to remain silent," she decided that was the best thing to do. But she could pray—and she did—for herself, for Scott, for Zac . . . and most of all, for Katlyn. She just couldn't die! Not until Natalie had asked her forgiveness for being so jealous. For not loving her with God's love. For not being a true friend. . . .

"This way, miss," the officer said after he'd pulled to a stop and was opening the back door for her.

She had to walk fast to keep up with his long strides as he hurried up the concrete steps of the brick building. Across the front—in huge, gold letters—was spelled out: POLICE STATION. Was he going to throw her in jail for being an accomplice to a crime? She wanted to ask the officer, but he seemed so detached. To him, this incident that had blasted her world apart was probably all in a night's work.

He held the door open, and she passed through. Just inside, Natalie paused, taking in the starkness of the large lobby. About halfway across the room was a long desk, much like a kitchen counter top—an ugly green Formica—behind which another officer was sitting.

"He can call someone for you." The policeman gestured to the officer who was talking on the phone, apparently taking down some kind of information, then turned and left her standing there.

Natalie had heard that prisoners were allowed "one phone call" after an arrest. But she wasn't being arrested. Was she? Her mind was churning. Whom should she call? Not anyone at home—it would be long distance from here. Besides, Dad would be at work, and Mom would be a basket case when she heard the news. Still, the Chanders . . . and the Lamberts had to be told. Dr. Lambert. She had to put a call through to Dr. Lambert. . . .

"I need to get in touch with a Dr. Lawrence Lambert at Lake Oakwood," Natalie told the officer behind the desk as soon as he was off the phone, "but I don't know the number."

She felt slightly relieved when he eyed her kindly, then reached for a telephone book. "The Lamberts went out for the evening with the parents of the girl who was"—Natalie swallowed hard—"was . . . hurt in the accident."

The officer ran his finger down a page, then glanced up with concern. "I don't see a listing for a Dr. Lambert."

"Oh, I'm sorry." Natalie felt a warm flush. How could she have been so *dumb*? "It's probably listed under Brysen—Martha Brysen. The lake house belongs to her."

"Brysen? Oh, the big house on the hill at Lake Oakwood." He flipped toward the front. "Here it is." He dialed the number, then handed the phone to Natalie.

"Better not mention the girl who was hurt," he cautioned her. "The hospital will inform her parents."

Natalie nodded. *Oh, please, let Cissy answer the phone, and not Martha Brysen!* "Oh, Mrs. Brysen," Natalie said, feeling a surge of disappointment at the familiar voice on the other end of the line. "This . . . this is . . . Natalie."

"Natalie? Where are you, dear? What's going on?"

"Is Dr. Lambert there?"

"No, he and Helen haven't come in yet." There was a pause, then Mrs. Brysen went on, more firmly now. "You just tell me this instant what this is all about."

Feeling like a first-grader—again—gazing up at the teacher towering over her, Natalie knew she could no longer be evasive. "We went downtown," she began miserably. "Zac drove the car up on a curb"—she stopped to clear her throat—"and into a building. . . ."

"Is he all right? Are *you* all right? And Scott? You haven't mentioned Scott."

"I'm okay . . . but we're at the police station."

"The police station? Why, whatever for?"

"Zac . . . was drinking. . . ." Natalie's voice trailed off weakly.

"Oh, Lord, help us!" Mrs. Brysen cried. "Wait, honey. I think they're home. Lawrence!"

Natalie could hear Mrs. Brysen hastily bringing her brother-in-law up to date. Then a woman's wail, "Oh no, no!" followed by Martha Brysen's voice again, lowered in a comforting tone, "Now, Helen, let's not think the worst. . . ."

Natalie glanced helplessly at the police officer, who filled a cup with water from the cooler and set it down on the counter. "Thank you." She took a sip to wet her dry mouth.

"Natalie?" came Dr. Lambert's deep, rumbling bass. "What's this about an accident?"

She felt another moment's relief. Maybe, now, someone would do something. She took a deep breath and launched into her story, giving him the key details.

"I'll be right there," he said briskly.

Natalie stared at the receiver as she handed it back to the officer. "Dr. Lambert is on his way."

No sooner had he hung up than the phone rang again. The policeman covered the mouthpiece and motioned her over to a chair in the corner. "You can wait over there."

Feeling shaky, Natalie settled gratefully onto the dark green vinyl. It was warm and sticky against her bare legs. How many criminals had sat here?

Looking around, she noticed a closed door and wondered where it led. Was Zac back there somewhere? And what was going on with Scott and Katlyn? A great weight closed over her chest, choking off her breath. She'd never felt so alone.

Her gaze fell on her fingers, tightly entwined on her lap, then traveled to her shirt front. *I'm not alone!*

Of course! She knew that. She'd believed in God all

her life. Then, when she was old enough to understand that she should invite His Son, Jesus Christ, into her heart, His Spirit had moved in, too. *He promised He'd always be with me . . . so He's here right now!* The thought was startling. *How could I have forgotten that? God's not just in heaven—He's here in my heart—sitting beside me, holding my hand, probably putting His arm around my shoulders. . . .*

Natalie squeezed her eyes shut, feeling the tears forming again. But this time, they were tears of release as the Spirit's comforting presence flooded her.

"I've seen that logo somewhere," the policeman said, bringing her thoughts back to the stark, sterile police lobby. "White Dove—is that a singing group?"

"No, sir, it's a church youth group."

The officer brightened. "That's right. The paper did a nice write-up on what you kids are doing over in Garden City—how you're helping the victims of the tornado."

Natalie nodded, grateful for a topic of conversation that would take her mind off the predicament she was in. "It started out as a program to encourage young people to stay sexually pure before marriage," she began, halfway embarrassed. "But it's been expanded to include living a pure life in every way." She flinched, realizing how far short of that goal she'd fallen in the past twenty-four hours. She tugged at her shirttail. "The white dove is a symbol of God's Spirit, who is love—pure love."

The officer regarded her thoughtfully for a long moment. Natalie tucked a flyaway strand of hair behind one ear. Maybe she had just *imagined* he seemed interested.

"Sounds like a great idea." His gaze took on a distant look. Then he focused on her again. "I have a fourteen-year-old son who needs to get involved in something like that for the summer."

"Really?" It seemed odd that the police officer would be sharing something so personal about his family. "I'd be glad to have my youth director send him some information, if you think he'd like to have it."

"I'll give you the address." He took out a business card and scribbled something on the back.

Natalie walked over and waited while he wrote. Who would have ever believed she'd be standing in a police station on a hot July night, witnessing about her faith to a perfect stranger?

He handed her the card. "That's the name of our church and the youth director. Maybe it would be better to send the information to him rather than directly to my son. He's pretty tough—doesn't think he needs . . . well, you understand how it is with parents and teenagers."

Natalie couldn't believe it. The man was actually speaking to her as an equal. She turned his card over and read the officer's name—Jim Burns. "It's been nice talking to you, Officer Burns."

"You too . . . Natalie."

He winked, and she felt a warm rush of pleasure. He certainly hadn't made her feel like a criminal. *We're friends . . . friends in Christ*, she sensed with a kind of awe. Despite the awful things that were going on around her—the uncertainty—she felt an unexplainable inner peace.

The officer inhaled deeply, then changed the subject. "You seem like a good kid. What were you doing with that guy?"

"He's my . . . friend's brother," she explained. "I haven't known him long, but I'd never seen him like that. He was acting so weird, we couldn't let him go off alone."

"Too bad you had to get mixed up in this."

"I guess that's what friends are for." She paused, realizing the importance of what she was saying. "What will happen to him?"

The officer spoke matter-of-factly. "He'll probably be held overnight in the drunk tank." He shrugged. "After that . . . it's up to the judge."

Even in his alcohol-induced stupor, Zac knew where he was. He'd passed the police station and the adjoining jail plenty of times in the past. But he'd never given the place more than a passing thought. Why should he? Jail had never been any part of his life—until now.

On the way, he'd heard the cop driving the cruiser radioing in the details of "the latest DUI." Now, they were pulling up at the back of the jail, with the station house right across the alley.

The cop led him inside. The minute he stepped inside the dimly lighted concrete building, Zac felt a wrench in his gut. The air was oppressive, hot and stale. He was taken down a narrow hallway with small cubicles on either side—bare, except for a table and a chair or two. At the end of the hall, they stepped out into an alley and through a door leading to the station house.

How did this happen? Where did they take Scott? And the girl? I didn't run up on that curb and hit her . . . did I? It was all a hazy blur, spinning around in his head. His heart thudded against his rib cage, echoing the hollow sound of his footsteps on the cement floor.

Shoving Zac into a small room, the arresting officer signaled the cop sitting at the desk. "He's all yours. Book him."

The second officer stood to his feet, scowling. "Another one? This place is crawling with these guys who get happy around the holidays." He produced a small piece of equipment attached to a hollow tube. "Blow into this."

Zac didn't argue but did as he was instructed.

"Turn around and hold on to the wall." The officer patted him down—searching for weapons, Zac supposed. *Funny*, he thought with grim humor, *the only weapon I had tonight was my car.*

"Take off your belt and give us your shoelaces."

"Shoela-shes?" Zac mumbled thickly. "Think I can do some damage with shoela-shes?" He complied with the request reluctantly.

"Okay. Now your wallet, anything you have in your pockets, and your watch," the officer recited blandly. "That gold chain around your neck, too."

"Look, thish stuff is mine. I have my rights, y'know."

"You have the right to remain silent, that's all. Either give us the items, or we'll take them. Your hide, too, if necessary."

Zac didn't put up any further resistance.

He allowed the officer to fingerprint him, then lead

him to another room with a table—bare except for a telephone—and one chair.

"You can make one phone call, buddy," the officer advised.

Zac stared at the phone. Whom could he call? His dad? Yeah, sure! *Hey, Dad, I'm drunk. I nearly killed my brother and maybe a girl. And I don't have any idea where Natalie got to.* Sure! He shook his head.

"Well, this is your chance, bud. If you don't want to call anyone, then let's go."

The cop took him down the hall and around a corner where a guard was approaching from the opposite direction. "In there."

Zac recoiled in disgust. Behind bars was a concrete room—gray walls, gray floor, gray benches lining the three walls. An open commode yawned against one side of the room. There was nothing more—except for fifteen or twenty drunks, all crammed into the small space.

"I can't go in there," Zac protested. "I'm . . . ah"—he searched for the word—"not old enough."

The officer double-checked the file he held in his hand. "Says here you're nineteen. Not old enough to drink, maybe, but you're drunk. So into the tank."

A guard unlocked the barred door, shoved him into the cell, and closed the door. Zac could hear the heavy clink of metal on metal as the lock slid into place behind him.

Twenty pairs of eyes were trained on the newest arrival. Curious eyes. Unfriendly eyes. Leering eyes.

"Hey, got us a cute one, ain't we?" came an obscene voice from somewhere in the crowded room.

There were a few snickers and a loud catcall or two.

"Pipe down in there, you creeps," growled the guard and moved off with the officer, leaving Zac utterly defenseless.

No one made way for him as Zac stumbled into the room. He made an attempt to step over an outstretched pair of legs, tripped, and fell to his hands and knees. Fearing the guy might attack him in this vulnerable position, Zac apologized profusely, then looked over to find that the man was out cold.

"Got lucky on that one," one guy said, and the snickers started up again.

Still on all fours, Zac crawled to the first vacant spot. Beneath him, the floor felt damp and slimy and smelled of sour vomit. Then he felt it coming. As soon as he began to gag, a path was cleared to the commode. Hanging over it, he heaved and retched, losing the contents of his stomach . . . and a whole lot more.

Pride. Dignity. The respect of his younger brother. And that wasn't all. In that awful moment of truth, the fog lifted, and Zac knew. If the girl he'd run down was dead, he might even have to pay with his own life!

Ten

Lawrence and Helen Lambert, looking pale and distraught, arrived at the police station soon after Natalie's call.

Dr. Lambert knelt in front of Natalie, visually checking for cuts and bruises, while Helen Lambert—chic in a smart linen suit, every hair in place—stood by, wringing her hands.

"Are you hurt anywhere, Natalie?"

"I'm fine, Dr. Lambert."

Satisfied from his cursory examination that she had sustained no serious injury, he rose. "We'll get you out of here in a little while."

"Have you seen Scott?"

"Not yet. I called the hospital, but they hadn't completed their preliminary work-up. They're to leave word with Martha." He sighed heavily, and Natalie thought she had never seen such a troubled expression. "In any event, we'll go by as soon as we see about Zac."

Helen Lambert's eyes were tragic pools of blue in her chalk white face. She followed her husband to the desk, shaking visibly.

The kind policeman behind the desk—Jim Burns—

123

had been joined by the arresting officer, bearing a legal pad and file folder. Briefly, he explained the confinement procedures that had been carried out and ended with the shocking news that Zac would not be leaving with them.

At this, Dr. Lambert flexed his jaw, his dark brows drawn together in a worried frown.

"M-may we see our son?" Mrs. Lambert's voice was shaking.

"Afraid not, ma'am," Officer Burns spoke up.

Dr Lambert glanced at his wife. "This is still officially the weekend, Helen—the holiday, you remember. There's little we can do before tomorrow."

A small cry escaped Helen Lambert's throat, and she blinked back tears. Bracing an elbow on one hand, she brought the other to her forehead, kneading the smooth skin with her fingers—as if she were in pain—as she listened to her husband's telephone conversation with her sister Martha.

Natalie held her breath. Judging from the look on Dr. Lambert's face, the news must not be good.

"I see . . . yes . . . Scott said *what*!"

What could Scott possibly have said to cause such a reaction? Natalie wondered. Then her spirits soared. At least he was conscious and able to communicate.

Dr. Lambert turned away from his wife, his body language clearly shutting her out. She appeared as if she might faint, then catching Natalie's eye, lifted her chin determinedly and walked over to the green seats. Perched on the edge, Helen Lambert wrapped her arms around herself and began to rock back and forth, moaning softly.

Natalie watched, not sure what to say or do.

Shortly, Mrs. Lambert seemed to realize that she was being observed and shrank back against the wall, as if trying to make herself invisible.

"Scott's going to be all right," Dr. Lambert reported after a call to the hospital. "But he has a nasty cut on his forehead. They're stitching it up now, so it will be a while before we can see him. He's in good hands. Jerry Vine is a good man."

Helen Lambert looked up, blinking her eyes owlishly. "I thought we were going to the hospital."

"Not just yet," he replied curtly.

Although Mrs. Lambert had perked up a little at the good news of Scott's condition, her eyes brightening, Natalie wondered why Dr. Lambert was still so stiff and formal. Shouldn't they be hugging each other, crying for joy in each other's arms?

Instead, the woman was avoiding her husband's stern gaze, her lips trembling. What was going on with these two?

Trailing them to the door, Natalie waved to Officer Burns.

"Goodbye, young lady," he called after her. "And thanks . . . for everything."

Dr. Lambert waited, holding the door open. Natalie hurried past him, following Helen Lambert down the steps. What was the problem, Natalie wondered, between Scott, his father, and this beautiful woman who looked as if she had everything money could buy—everything, that is, except her confidence and her family?

On the way back to the lake house, Natalie kept

quiet. Although she was curious, it wasn't her place to ask what had happened with Zac. She glanced into the mirror above the dash. Dr. Lambert's face was a stony mask. He stared straight ahead, his gaze never wavering from the road.

Sitting beside him on the front seat, Helen Lambert began to weep softly. "Scott doesn't want to see me, does he?"

There was no reply.

The cry became a wail. "My boys! My poor boys! And it's all *my* fault! *I'm* to blame!"

———

When Natalie and the Lamberts returned to the lake house, Martha Brysen and Cissy were waiting, concerned and eager to hear more about the accident. Mrs. Lambert sank down onto the plush sofa, and Martha Brysen sat beside her, patting her hand, waiting expectantly for someone to speak.

All of a sudden, Natalie's legs gave way, and she stumbled over to a chair. No doubt she would be expected to answer questions about the accident. After all, she was the only eyewitness present. How many times would she have to rehash the whole ugly scenario? And who else would want to know? The Chanders? The media? Some judge?

Dr. Lambert seemed to sense her distress. "Natalie's been through quite an ordeal tonight. We can hear her side of the story later. Right now, I have several calls to make."

At that moment, the phone rang.

Lawrence Lambert picked up the receiver, listening

intently. "I really appreciate this, Don."

While her uncle listened, Cissy sat on the arm of Natalie's chair. "Don Hamilton," she explained. "He's one of the hospital administrators here, like my dad is in Garden City. He knows Uncle Larry and said he'd call back when he had more information about Scott."

Natalie nodded and leaned forward to hear Dr. Lambert's end of the conversation.

"Yes, I see. Yes, I know I'd tell my patients to stay home and rest. But who ever listens to a doctor's advice?" he said in a lame attempt at lightheartedness. "I'll go to the hospital right away. Do you know anything about the Chander girl? Yes, I'd appreciate it if you'd phone as soon as you've heard."

"What . . . Chander girl?" Cissy asked Natalie.

From Cissy's quizzical expression, it was plain that she hadn't heard all the news. Natalie tried to break it gently. "Katlyn."

"Katlyn?" Cissy squeaked.

Mrs. Brysen appeared equally confused.

"Zac's car . . . struck her . . . and pinned her legs against a storefront."

There was a moment while Natalie's startling statement registered. Then there was a gasp from Martha Brysen, while Cissy stared down at Natalie, her mouth wide.

"What else can go wrong?" Mrs. Lambert covered her face with her hands and moaned.

When Dr. Lambert got off the phone, he seemed somewhat relieved. "Well, that's good news, at least. Don says the X-ray shows that Scott does not have a concussion. His cut's pretty deep, though—it required sixteen stitches. They want to keep him at the hospital for a couple of days for observation."

"We must go to him," Martha Brysen said with a determined set of her chin.

"No." Dr. Lambert halted her before she could reach for her purse on the coffee table. "Don said Scott is quite emotional. They've given him something to calm him down and help him sleep."

Then he inhaled deeply and stared off into some distant thought. "Don wasn't able to learn anything about Katlyn, except that her condition is critical."

"Oh, thank the Lord!" Natalie blurted, then realized how that must have sounded. "What I mean is . . . I thought she was . . ."

As if on cue, the phone rang again, and Dr. Lambert grabbed it. The one-sided conversation was brief. "I understand," he said in a low tone as the color drained from his face.

Slowly, he replaced the receiver in its cradle, then looked from one stricken face to the next. "I guess I don't need to tell you who that was." A searing pain burned in Dr. Lambert's eyes. "Katlyn is alive and in surgery, but she's lost a lot of blood. Chander talked to me only long enough to make it clear that he wants nothing to do with any member of my family."

He paused, his mouth twitching. "And he wants . . . the maximum penalty for the one who did this to his daughter."

With a cry of alarm, Helen Lambert jumped up off the couch and ran down the hallway to her room.

"Martha, will you make some coffee? It's going to be a long night." Dr. Lambert massaged the muscles at the base of his skull, then lifted a tragic face to his sister-in-law. "Scott doesn't want to see Helen. Maybe you could talk with her after I'm gone. I'll call my attorney from the upstairs sitting room."

He was on the way up when he paused and looked back at the two girls. "Cissy, would you get some pajamas and a change of clothes for Scott, please?"

Mrs. Brysen headed for the kitchen, Cissy and Natalie for the boys' room. Just inside the bedroom door, they stopped short. Helen Lambert had dragged a chair across the floor to the bookcase and was tugging a liquor bottle from behind some books on the top shelf.

Startled by the girls' sudden appearance, she yelled at them. "Get out!"

Cissy's eyes were wide. "Aunt Helen?"

Natalie backed away, trying to make herself inconspicuous.

"Did you hear me? I said to get out!"

The two lost no time in stepping into the hallway.

"So *that's* her problem," Cissy whispered to Natalie. Spinning on her heel, Cissy raced for the stairs, leaving Natalie, frozen to the spot, in the downstairs hallway.

When Cissy returned with her uncle, the two girls hung back, holding on to the door facing while he rushed inside. He hesitated inside the door—statue-still.

Helen had climbed down and was taking a few unsteady steps, pausing to grasp the dresser for balance. "Don't you see? I *need* this right now!" she blared at her husband. Her eyes were wild. "Don't you understand that? My son's in jail! He may be there for the rest of his life! And we all know who's to blame."

Dr. Lambert waited, listening.

"Well? Aren't you going to stop me?" Helen dared him. "Say something? Call me names?"

"No. Not anymore." His tone was flat, lifeless. "It's over, Helen. I'm finished. I give up. Take your bottle. Drink it. There's nothing more I can do for you."

Like a trapped animal, Mrs. Lambert looked around helplessly, then tossed her head in defiance. She ran into the bathroom with the bottle, slammed the door, and locked it behind her.

Since her uncle had made no move to reason with her aunt, Cissy rushed to the door. "Aunt Helen, please don't do this. We don't blame you for what Zac did."

"Shut up! Shut up and leave me alone!"

With her hands pressed against the bathroom door, Cissy began to cry. Natalie walked over and patted her friend's shoulder. "Mrs. Lambert," Natalie began, praying she wouldn't make things worse, "you have another son, remember? The one in the hospital needs you, too."

Dr. Lambert opened his mouth as if to speak, but no words came. Only the tears streaming down his face told of his suffering. Silently, the three looked toward the closed door, where they could hear Helen Lambert sobbing uncontrollably.

Then the sobs died away, and there was silence— an ominous silence.

Dr. Lambert went to the phone in his bedroom across the hall and called the clinic. "This is Lawrence

Lambert." He paused, listening, then, "Yes, I'll bring her back in the morning."

He closed his eyes as if summoning strength within himself, then turned a sad gaze on Cissy and Natalie, who were observing through the open door. "I'm sorry you two had to witness this. Natalie, I'm sorry about everything that has happened this evening. As much as I regret it, I think it's time we called your parents."

At the sound of a loud thump from the boys' bathroom across the hall, they hurried back to see the knob turning. The door opened slowly, and they waited, almost afraid of what they would see.

But when Helen Lambert appeared, she was empty-handed. Her face was wet, her eyes puffy, but there was something admirable in the way she lifted her chin and spoke with confidence, despite the tremor in her voice. "My sons need me."

For the first time Natalie could recall, Helen Lambert looked at her, really looked at her—before she turned her gaze on her husband. "I understand why you feel you've had it with me, Larry. I really don't know how you've stood it this long. I'm so . . . sorry." Tears rained down the smooth cheeks. "And you're right. You *can't* help me."

Wearily, he brushed past her and into the bathroom. He picked up the bottle from the wastebasket. It was full, the seal unbroken. "You didn't drink any, Helen," he said wonderingly.

She shook her head and leaned more heavily on the dresser top. "Oh, I know you think I'm playing some sort of game, Larry. I've done it too many times before. Why should you believe that things are different now?"

Natalie darted a glance at Cissy, whose eyes were wide with apprehension. Looking at Dr. Lambert, she saw his skepticism, the sad, tolerant expression on his face. His nostrils flared slightly as if he were having difficulty controlling his emotions.

Mrs. Lambert drew in a deep breath, looked down at the dresser, and lifted a small object. "Look," she said, holding up the little dove that had been lying there with Scott's pocket change. "This was the thing that finally got through to me. I heard you talking about the little pocket dove that had made such a difference the night Cissy was caught in the tornado. How it reminded her of God and His Spirit. . . . I thought it was a lovely story." She addressed Natalie now. "Then I saw you and Scott wearing those shirts."

Natalie and Cissy stared at her, each wondering where this was going.

"I supposed it was a nice little club for Christian young people—a sweet motto, if you cared for that sort of thing. But I had my own little club."

She paced the room, turning to face them, grasping the dove in her hand. "I'll tell you something I've never confessed before. I've never really wanted to quit drinking. Most of my friends do it. Even many of the doctors and their wives in our circle of friends drink socially." She watched her husband's reaction carefully. He flinched.

"In fact, drinking has been an escape for me—from whom or what, I really don't know." She frowned thoughtfully. "I guess that's something I'll have to explore. I do know that it turned into something more than a social custom—it became a monster that controlled me, almost consumed me. It . . . may have been responsible for taking the life of an innocent young girl—" Her voice broke again. "And it has ruined one son's life . . . and turned my other son against me"— Helen Lambert continued to hold Dr. Lambert's gaze—"not to mention my wonderful husband."

He still didn't make a move toward her.

She stiffened her shoulders and went on bravely. "But I've made a decision—perhaps the most important of my life. I'm going to fight to regain Scott's respect, Larry. And I have another son I must fight to save. But first, I must save myself."

She looked from one to the other. "The thing I'm learning is . . . that I *can't* save myself. Only God can do that. And if He doesn't, then I have no hope at all. You see," she dropped her head, tears dripping onto the floor, "I'm a complete mess. . . . I'm an . . . alcoholic."

There was not a sound in the room except for her quiet sobbing.

When Dr. Lambert took a step toward his wife, Natalie held her breath. She had never seen such a look on a man's face—pity, mingled with love and hope— as if his heart had been wrenched from his body and was being bared to the world. "Helen?" He held out his hand to her.

Helen Lambert lifted her tear-streaked face.

"That's the first step . . . to healing," he whispered brokenly.

What happened next was a dizzying blur. In one more swift step, they were in each other's arms, crying bitterly, murmuring words of love and confession and forgiveness.

Natalie and Cissy tiptoed out of the room. Neither of the Lamberts even noticed.

Eleven

On Tuesday morning, Scott felt worse than he had the night before. He was sore all over, and although the doctors had assured him that he had no broken ribs, they couldn't prove it by *him*.

"I don't want to see anyone," he growled to a nurse when a visitor burst into the private room where he had been sent after his cut was stitched in the ER.

"Not even your old dad?" Lawrence Lambert was grinning from ear to ear. "But what's this about no breakfast? There are no restrictions on your diet, son. So what'll it be? Belgian waffles? Eggs Benedict? A Big Mac? Place your order, and I'll serve it myself, *monsieur*." He grabbed a towel from the rack and swept it over one arm, making a low bow, in parody of a maitre d'.

Scott raised a brow suspiciously. He hadn't seen his dad acting like this since . . . the old days. He turned away from his father's dopey antics and looked out the window.

Even the bright midmorning sun did nothing to lift Scott's spirits. He felt as though he'd been sucked into the Black Hole of Calcutta. No, it wasn't food he wanted. "I . . . don't want to live at home anymore, Dad."

Lawrence dragged up a chair by the bedside. "Scott, I know you're blaming your mother for all this. And believe me, she's blaming herself. You said you didn't want to see her . . . but she came with me anyway, just in case. She's outside in the hall and—"

"No, Dad!" Scott interrupted him. "No way." His mother's problem had gone beyond herself now. It had drawn all of them in—like the vortex of the tornado that had descended on Garden City—spinning out of control. Her drinking had ruined Zac's life and now Katlyn's and—if he lost Natalie—his too. Just when Scott was hoping things were getting better, they'd taken a nasty turn for the worse. No. He wouldn't see his mom. And that was final.

"I thought we'd agreed to give your mother another chance, son. She admits she can't lick her problem without help—*God's* help."

There was a pleading note in his father's voice that Scott had not heard before. "Why did she say that, Dad? Ha! Don't bother answering that. I'll bet I know." His tone dripped with sarcasm. He knew it must be like rubbing salt in an open wound, but he couldn't stop himself. "You threatened to divorce her again, didn't you?"

"I told her the marriage was over when I saw her with a bottle in her hand last night, yes," his father admitted with a shrug of his shoulders. "But . . ."

Scott nodded knowingly. "Dad, you know she always promises anything—always says she's sorry, says she'll never drink again—every time you give her an ultimatum."

Lawrence sighed, plowing his hand through his silvering hair. "Yes, I know. But when she came home this time, I told her it would be the last time if she starts drinking again. She knows I mean it. And last night—in the middle of everything that's going on—when she was most tempted to turn to the bottle—she turned it down. She didn't take that drink, son."

"But I always expect her to, Dad. I've tried not to, but I keep waiting and wondering when she'll do it again. I can't trust her. I've tried. I've really tried."

There was a long pause. Scott couldn't bear to look at his dad. It would be too painful—worse than his cuts and bruises—to see the look of defeat on his father's face.

"I know you have, son," Lawrence said wearily. "But this time"—his tone brightened—"I really think it's going to be different. Your mother has admitted that even rehab can't help her unless she's willing to turn her problem over to God."

Scott was still skeptical. "Sorry, Dad. I wish I could believe that. But it's too late. She's gone too far this time. What about Zac? What's going to happen to him? And Katlyn?"

His dad didn't have an answer for that one.

"And what about Natalie?" Scott choked. "Even if she wanted to, her parents would never let her near us again. You know what a neat family they are. They're not like . . ." His voice trailed off miserably, and he felt sick, knowing what this must be doing to his father.

"Us?" his father finished for him. Lawrence leaned nearer the bed and looked into Scott's face. "I think there's something you ought to know, son. When I called the Ainsworths last night, I told them everything. I even told them about your mother's alcohol problem. Told them I wouldn't blame them at all if they didn't want Natalie exposed to the kind of problems we're having." He waited, seeing Scott's look of disbelief. "Would you like to know what Jim Ainsworth said?"

Scott wasn't sure he would.

But his dad went on, "He said that this is a time for Christians to show their love for one another—not turn their backs. He reminded me that even the people closest to God can sometimes fail. Simon Peter denied his Lord. King David took another man's wife, then had her husband killed—" Lawrence paused, his voice rising in his enthusiasm, then dropping again as he gazed into Scott's dark eyes.

"We're all human beings, capable of doing wrong. But there's no sin so black that it can't be forgiven. No person who's fallen so low that he—or she—can't change with God's help. . . . That *is* what we say we believe, isn't it, son?"

Scott let out a hoot that ended in a choked cry. "That's what we *say* we believe."

Lawrence gripped Scott's shoulder. "It's tough when it hits home, and we're put to the test, right?" he went on confessionally. "After last night, I know something about that."

"Yes, sir." Scott was tired of fighting it.

"Sorry you're having to deal with this while you're recovering from the accident, son. But I want you to know I'm proud of you. You make me feel"—he paused and wiped his eyes—"that I haven't completely failed as a father."

Scott couldn't stand it when his dad got all emotional. "Aw, Dad, you're the greatest. But you're trying to lay a guilt trip on me, aren't you?" He struggled for a lighter tone. "Well, flattery might just get you somewhere."

Lawrence got up and perched on the edge of the bed, reaching over to draw Scott into a hard embrace. "I love you, son. And . . . I need you."

Scott let the tears go, not ashamed when they trickled onto his father's shirt front. "Love you, too, Dad."

They drew apart and Lawrence rose. "Scott, I'll respect your feelings if you do decide to live with Martha for a while and if you won't agree to see your mother right away. But, please, do one thing for me. . . ."

Scott braced himself. "Sure, Dad."

"Pray about it."

"I have prayed, Dad." He gave a gesture of helplessness. "I've prayed about Mom for years."

Lawrence held his son's gaze. "Then it's time for another confession. I haven't been the spiritual leader this home has needed. Oh, I've prayed from time to time, gone to church. But I've been negligent about really committing my family to God. Well, things are going to be different from now on, I can promise you that."

He rose and paced the room, pausing at the foot of Scott's bed. "I've released your mother into the care of the Great Physician. Zac too. It's out of my hands. I can't change either of them. But He can. All we can do now is pray . . . and trust God to work."

Scott really wanted to believe that. But he was still not convinced. "That won't be so easy to do."

"Maybe not. But it's the only thing we have left."

Scott put his hand to the bandage on his head and blinked his eyes against the dull ache in his head—echoed in the painful throbbing of his heart.

Obviously noting his son's discomfort, Lawrence was the professional again. "I'll send in a nurse to give you something for the pain. Oh, and by the way, Natalie mentioned that she'd like to stop by this afternoon . . . if you're up to having visitors, that is."

Scott tried to hide the sudden elation that swept through him. But he doubted that he'd been successful when he looked up and saw the twinkle in his dad's eyes. "Well, the least I can do is apologize to her," he explained in his own defense.

His dad's expression sobered. "Sure. I understand, son. She really is a remarkable young woman. Even your aunt Martha—the eternal censor—seems to think so."

Scott laughed, feeling better than he'd felt all day. He winced at the sudden stab of pain in his head. But he was still smiling when his dad left the room.

Scott didn't intend to be lying in bed like some invalid when Natalie came to see him, although his head still hurt and he'd felt a little dizzy earlier when the nurses had helped him up to walk a few steps.

So he was fully dressed—shorts, T-shirt, even his sneakers—and was propped up in bed on top of the covers when she knocked on the door and peeked in. It wasn't his head that was throbbing this time. His heart picked up speed until it was hammering like he'd been given a shot of adrenaline.

She looked terrific! Why hadn't he noticed how really beautiful she was? She'd dressed up for him too—or was that wishful thinking?—in a short navy-and-white-striped dress. Her hair, gleaming as if it had caught all the summer sunlight, flowed down to her shoulders in soft waves.

"Pardon me for not standing," he said. "I might faint again." He *didn't* mean from the gash on his head. But she must not know that.

"Oh, Scott," the smile left her pretty face for a moment as her deep blue eyes sparked with sympathy. "I'm so sorry you're hurt. But your dad says you're going to be okay. You are, aren't you?" She sat in a chair near the bed and set down the bag she was carrying.

He decided to milk it a little. "Lost a lot of blood from the cut on my head, you know." He touched the spot gingerly. "Quite a lump there. They want to keep me here for a while to make sure everything *stays* okay. Actually"—he crossed his ankles and laced his fingers behind his head, grinning—"I really ought to enjoy this while it lasts. I seem to be getting preferential treatment—all the doctors in the family, I guess. And I think Aunt Martha owns a wing of this hospital, too."

There was that great smile again—Natalie's even, white teeth against her tanned face. A thought occurred to Scott, and he frowned in concern. "But how about you, Natalie? Were you hurt at all?"

"Not really. Got thrown around some, and I'm a little sore. But otherwise fine."

He wanted to say she looked *better* than fine.

The mega-smile faded. "Katlyn's in pretty bad

shape, though," Natalie went on.

Scott nodded. "Dad says she's critical."

"Your mom said her legs are crushed, and she's still in a coma."

"My mom? When did you talk to her?"

Natalie seemed surprised. "In the waiting room."

"She's in the waiting room? Now?"

Natalie nodded.

"Did she tell you I won't see her?"

"Yes . . . but I wondered . . . why not?"

He felt ashamed. "You don't want to hear it!"

"I do . . . if you want to tell me about it."

Scott propped himself into a more comfortable position on the pillows. "I'd hoped no one would find out about my mom. But since you already know. . . ." He launched into his sad story, not quite sure how much to share with Natalie. She was a special girl, all right, but she was human. How much could she take before she turned away in disgust?

"Mom's been an alcoholic for years. She tried to deny it for a long time. We went along. I knew my parents drank socially—or used to—so it was easy to tell myself that she wasn't really drunk, just a little high, all those times she . . ." He didn't finish, but let Natalie fill in the blanks. "But I began to realize how serious the problem was when Zac was a senior in high school." Scott gazed out the window, recalling the incident.

"Zac came home drunk from a party once, and both my folks read him the riot act. Zac said he'd only had a few drinks, that he could handle it. Then my dad began to lecture him. 'You never know, son,' he said.

'You don't realize the danger. Alcoholism becomes chronic for some people, a disease. Better stop before it gets hold of you.'

"Then my brother jumped up from the table, madder than a hornet. Told Dad not to preach to him. 'You think I'm going to turn out like Mom, don't you?' he said. 'Well, where do you think I got the booze in the first place? From one of her hiding places, that's where! Think I don't know I've got a drunk for a mother? Well, everyone in town knows!' Then he stormed out of the house."

There was a long silence while Scott composed himself. He'd heard his dad run after Zac, his mother pleading with him not to leave. Then, when everything was quiet, Scott had heard her go into the library and close the door. He'd heard a loud pop, like the cork from a bottle, and he'd known what she was up to. She hadn't come out, even when his dad and brother had returned later that night.

"The next morning at breakfast—while Mom was sleeping off another hangover—Zac told Dad and me he was really sorry, that he'd never take another drink, that he'd learned his lesson. We believed him because we wanted to. Guess he just learned to hide it as well as Mom always did."

Scott picked at a loose thread on the sleeve of his T-shirt. "I wouldn't blame you, Nat, if you didn't want to have anything to do with my family again."

Natalie gave him a moment, then moved to the edge of her seat. "Scott," she began softly.

He looked up, dreading what she might say.

"Scott, I like you for yourself. I know you're a

Christian who's trying to live by God's rules, and that's what counts with me. And there's nothing wrong with your family that alcohol hasn't caused." Seeing his expression brighten, she hurried on. "I don't know your mother very well, but I felt she was really sincere last night about wanting to change."

Scott nodded. "I know. She's very convincing. We've been fooled before. She's always sorry when she's caught. But then the same thing happens all over again. She has bottles stashed everywhere, and when the pressure builds—whatever it is—she becomes a different person . . . like Zac last night. And you know what happened to him. . . ."

There was a moment of heartbreaking silence as they thought about Zac, still in jail, and Katlyn, hovering between life and death in the Intensive Care Unit of the hospital.

"What would you do if the situation were reversed?" Natalie continued. "What if this happened to my family?"

He looked at her as if he thought she were crazy. "*Your* family? No way. You guys are perfect."

"But we're *not* perfect. And it could happen. Or something just as awful. *No one's* perfect."

She reached out and touched his arm, and he grabbed her hand, hanging on for dear life. He couldn't say a word. If he opened his mouth, he was afraid he'd cry again. And he just couldn't let Natalie see him like that.

Finally, with a sly grin on her face, Natalie wiggled her hand a little and tugged it from Scott's grip. In one lightning-fast move, she reached into the bag, picked something up, and threw it at him.

At first glance, it looked like a giant tarantula. Scott reacted with a sharp outcry. But he caught it and then broke out laughing. It was a stuffed monkey with long, floppy arms and a mouth that opened to reveal cloth teeth and a bright red tongue.

"Just what I've always wanted, Nat," he joked. "How did you know?" He cuddled the animal close to his heart, wishing it could be Natalie he was holding.

———

Scott felt much better as the day wore on. He hadn't lost Natalie after all, though he wasn't exactly sure how she felt about him. Still, he believed that sharing his family problems had strengthened their friendship. He thanked God for that.

By late afternoon, he was feeling so much stronger that he decided to follow his dad's suggestion and pray about his decision to move away from home and live with Aunt Martha. And he'd better pray again for Katlyn and her family . . . and Zac. But every time he closed his eyes, he was interrupted. It was either a nurse taking his temperature; a doctor shining a flashlight into his eyes to check again for possible concussion; or someone delivering flowers.

By suppertime, he'd recovered much of his balance, strength, and appetite. Even the hospital food tasted pretty good. It wasn't a porterhouse steak or burgers and fries, but he was ravenous, and he wolfed it down. After supper, he decided to sneak out of his room, bypass the waiting room in case his mom was there, and take the elevator down to the chapel.

The ride down made him light-headed, and after getting off the elevator, he held on to the wall and inched his way to a door marked with a cross and the word CHAPEL in gold letters. The door swung back easily and silently. He stood inside, feeling much the same as he did when walking from brilliant sunlight into a darkened movie theater. He'd have to give his eyes a minute or two to adjust. He wondered if he'd taken on too much too soon, for now his head was swimming.

When he could focus again, he made out a lighted cross on the far wall. Seeing several rows of seats, he slid into the one nearest the door and leaned his head back against the wall. The wound was throbbing again—probably from all the activity.

Closing his eyes, he soaked in the peace, the stillness. It was cool in here, too. After a while he began to relax, feeling his stiff muscles responding to the serenity around him. He knew he wasn't alone. God was always with him. He'd just sit here a little longer and rest before making his way down to the front where he could kneel in front of the cross.

As he rested, his mind replayed the events of the past couple of days—the accident, the few horrifying images at the scene that had registered in his clouded mind, the fear that still remained . . . Zac . . . Katlyn . . . He really ought to try to see about Katlyn for himself, find out how she was doing. If he had any strength left after this outing, he'd go by ICU on his way back to his room.

What was that?

It was such a tiny sound, almost a squeak. He

smiled, thinking of the proverbial "church mouse."

He heard it again—slightly louder this time. Without opening his eyes, he figured that since this was a chapel, someone else had come in to pray.

The sound became a sob. Then a flood of choked words he couldn't understand. He opened his eyes and, in the dimly lighted room, he saw the hazy figure of a woman, kneeling at the front. With an anguished sob, she fell forward on the altar, praying aloud.

Had someone died? Maybe it was Mrs. Chander—Katlyn's mother. . . . Scott's lips began to tremble. *I have so much. So many blessings. Even with my mom's and my brother's problem, we still have one another. . . .*

Scott closed his eyes again, but he couldn't shut out that woman's grief. He felt guilty, concentrating on his own problems when this poor soul was obviously going through some great crisis. *God, help me to stop dwelling on my heartache, my needs, my problems. Dad needs me. And Natalie still likes me . . . at least, as a friend. Maybe this woman has no one. Maybe she doesn't even know you. Use me to reach out and help others. And, God, help me begin right now.*

Scott pushed himself out of his seat, no longer feeling his sore muscles, his aching head. He had to let that woman know she was not alone, that someone cared about what she was going through. He'd pray with her. He'd even cry with her. . . .

As he got closer, her muffled words became clearer. The prayer seemed all tangled up, though he could tell she was praying for someone who had been hurt. Then she was begging for forgiveness, asking God to heal *her.*

Scott didn't know if she'd listen, but he wanted to tell her that she didn't have to beg God. God was always standing by to help. All she had to do was accept it.

Maybe she'll think I'm just a kid and have no business butting in. For a moment he hung back. Then, absolutely certain God wanted him to speak to her, Scott moved ahead. *I've got to quit thinking of myself and think about someone else for a change.*

The room spun dizzily as he reached the altar. He stopped until his head cleared. Then he fell to his knees and put his arm around the woman's thin shoulders. He could feel her body quivering with her suffering. A great shudder coursed through her body.

"Ma'am . . ." he began, hoping the Lord would put the next words in his mouth.

Slowly, with small gasps, the woman quieted and she lifted her head.

Scott's vision was still hazy, but as the woman turned to face him, he recognized the familiar profile. "Mom?"

"Scott!" she sobbed, burrowing her head into his chest. "Oh, Scott!"

Twelve

Zac came out of his sporatic dozing slowly, slitting one eye only to see if he could tolerate the light of day. The source of his irritation was a small, grease-streaked window through which a shaft of sunlight was filtering into the dim cell. Or maybe it was the stench—overpowering this morning—that had brought him back to consciousness.

Somehow—Zac wasn't sure how—he'd managed to scrounge a place for himself on the hard floor the last two nights and had dropped off for a few hours of oblivion. But he was awake now, and feeling all the misery he'd tried to drown two nights before.

He glanced around quickly to get his bearings. Several of the guys were still out. One was heaving up his insides over the commode. A few others were arguing loudly in the corner. What a pit!

When he finally opened both eyes, he felt the pain—like a hammer blow to the skull. Man! He blinked his eyes shut, holding his head in both hands. He was going to die. Whether it was caused by the alcohol and the accident or two nights in the drunk tank, the pain was terrible. A guy couldn't live long with pain like this.

The scrape of metal hinges grated across his raw nerves as the cell door swung open. "Lambert, Zachary T. Someone to see ya."

Zac stumbled to his feet, holding on to the wall with one hand, still cradling his head in the other.

"Come on, punk. I ain't got all day." The guard spat a stream of tobacco juice onto the stained concrete floor and stood aside to let Zac pass.

He followed blindly, feet dragging. It wasn't that he didn't welcome the idea of being out of that stinking hole, but the pain—even the sound of his own footsteps sounded like pistol shots in his ears.

Zac was escorted to another small room. Through bleary eyes, he made out the figures of a couple sitting at a table. They sprang to their feet when he entered. His mother was crying; his dad merely looked grim.

"Zac, I'm so sorry about all this," she was murmuring. "So sorry."

The one word his dad choked out was loaded with emotion. "Son . . ."

Zac ducked his head, twisting away from them. The last thing he wanted to do was look his parents in the eye.

"Son," Lawrence persisted, "sit down a minute. We've posted bond, and you're free to leave with us. But first, we've got to talk."

Zac vaguely registered his father's deep voice, full of anguish, as he spelled out the terms of Zac's release. Five thousand dollars bond . . . court hearing set one month from today . . . DUI with personal injury and property damage . . . possible felony charges. . . .

"We're facing a tough battle, son. And if Katlyn . . . well, it could be vehicular homicide we're looking at. . . ."

That's where Zac's brain cut out. *I don't want to hear any more.* . . .

"But, Zac, your mother and I are here for you. We're standing by . . . whatever it takes . . . for as long as it takes."

———

The atmosphere was strained when Natalie and Cissy joined Martha Brysen on the balcony for breakfast. No one had much to say. Even a bite of Rita Dunn's great cinnamon rolls tasted like a mouthful of sawdust.

"Lawrence and Helen have gone into town without waiting to eat," Martha explained. "They're eager to find out more about Zac and Scott, of course, and will let us know as soon as they learn anything."

Martha stirred her coffee absently, looking out on the lake. Natalie followed her gaze. Not a ripple disturbed the placid surface. To the visible eye, the mirror-bright water appeared perfectly calm and serene. Yet underneath, in the dark depths, lurked unknown danger—like those submerged logs Dr. Lambert had warned them about on their first day here. *Funny,* Natalie thought. *Life is just like that.*

"I suppose we were all wrong," Martha spoke aloud, more to herself than to Cissy and Natalie. "None of us wanted to admit that Helen might really have a serious drinking problem." She paused and took a sip of coffee.

"When Mama and Papa died, it was up to me to carry on. And I did the best I could with my two younger sisters. But it wasn't enough. I didn't know the Lord back then, didn't know that our heavenly Father would have helped me . . . if I'd just asked Him." She sighed.

"Helen was always the prettiest and daintiest of the three girls, had a delicate constitution—high-strung, you might say. So when she began acting peculiar after she and Lawrence married, we just assumed it was her nature. Maybe it was the alcohol all along."

"What about Zac?" Cissy spoke quietly. "Does that mean he's an alcoholic, too?"

Martha shook her head sadly. "I don't know. It may be that his body chemistry—like his mother's—can't cope with stimulants. Or maybe he just had too much to drink this time and lost control. We can only hope this will be a warning to him. We've tended to lock the truth away in a closet rather than bring it out in the open. Family pride, I suppose."

Natalie's heart went out to the woman. She'd never seen the confident Martha Brysen like this.

"But that's all behind us now. I've prayed plenty since I came to know the Lord in later life"—Martha brought up her chin in that familiar posture of determination Natalie knew so well—"and He won't desert us now. Maybe it took something like this to wake us all up."

The shrill ring of the telephone broke into Martha's somber monologue. Cissy ran to answer it and came back to report the latest news from the Lamberts. "Zac is out of jail on bond, and Scott is being released from the hospital later this morning. Aunt Helen and Uncle Larry will wait for him. Then they'll be coming back here around lunchtime."

"In that case," Martha began, picking up her coffee cup and plate and bustling toward the door, "we'll need to tell Rita to whip up something special for a homecoming meal."

———

When the phone rang an hour later, it was for Natalie.

"I want to know everything, and I mean *everything*—don't leave out a single word!" insisted an excited voice on the other end of the line.

"Ruthie Ryan, you nut!" Natalie was astonished. "What are you doing, calling me long distance? My parents are coming for me tonight, and we'll be home tomorrow!"

"Oh, I know, I know. They told me. But I couldn't wait another minute. You're in all the papers!"

Natalie couldn't help chuckling at her friend's latest exaggeration. "Ruthie, we only have *one* newspaper in Garden City."

"You know what I mean—you're in every *issue*!" Natalie could just see the big, brown eyes widening in dismay. "So quit stalling and give. What's the real scoop?"

Natalie filled her in on the accident—skipping some of the more gruesome details—and ending on a positive note. "But Scott's much better. He—and Zac and the Lamberts—will be here soon."

At the thought of seeing Scott again, Natalie's heart

lifted. The way he'd looked at her yesterday still left her weak. And the grip he'd had on her hand made her think he was beginning to care for her—at least a little.

"Nat?" Ruthie's tone was suspicious. "There's something different about your voice. You're in love, aren't you?"

Natalie was grateful that Ruthie couldn't see the blush that flooded her cheeks. "What are you talking about?"

"I'm not your best friend for nothing. What you *don't* say usually says more than what you *do* say! But you wanna know what I think?"

Ruthie was nothing if not persistent, Natalie thought fondly. "Shoot."

"I think it's just too dangerous for you two to be together. First, you had that hair-raising experience together in the tornado. Now a close call in a car accident. That's two strikes. Three strikes, and you're out!"

"You're crazy, Ruthie Ryan!" Natalie exploded in a release of laughter. "Tell me about Sean. Are you two still seeing each other as much as ever?"

"Oh, that Sean. He hasn't called me since the concert he *didn't* take me to. Guess he's really working hard." She sounded disgusted. "What about Katlyn?"

The mood shifted abruptly. "I haven't heard yet today. But last night she was still in a coma."

"Seriously, Nat. Maybe God is trying to tell you something through all this."

Natalie shrugged it off. But it played on her mind even after she hung up.

She knew God had given people free rein to be as

destructive or constructive as they chose to be. But He had also given warnings and rules. He didn't treat people like puppets on a string.

Zac hadn't been doing the will of God the night of the accident. But God could turn things around for him, and good could still come of it, just as good could come of the destructive tornado. But maybe it was the *secret* storms—the ones that swirled and churned beneath the surface—that did the most damage, Natalie pondered.

Natalie was convinced that God didn't hurt people in order to get their attention. It was people who hurt each other when they wouldn't listen to Him.

She sighed, feeling the heaviness of her thoughts. All she'd wanted to do was have a carefree summer— have a little fun—be what her mom often referred to as "footloose and fancy free."

Well, I am free, she decided. *Free to choose right or wrong. I have God's Word to help me know what's right, and His Spirit to help me do it. But if I fail,* she thought wonderingly, *I also have God's forgiveness and can pick up the pieces and start over . . . just like Helen Lambert is doing.*

———

When the Lamberts arrived, Zac looked awful— dark stubble on his chin, tousled hair, rumpled T-shirt that reeked of sweat and vomit. He swept by them without speaking to shower before lunch while Dr. Lambert explained.

"Zac is out on five thousand dollars bond, but there will be a hearing in a month. He could spend the best of his years in prison if"—his voice dropped to a near whisper—"the Chander girl doesn't make it, that is."

No one was very hungry, in spite of the excellent meal Rita laid out, picnic style, on the long dining table. They ate in shifts, taking their plates to different parts of the house—the Lamberts, Martha Brysen, and Cissy to the kitchen table to discuss the situation; Scott and Natalie to the balcony overlooking the lake. Zac would eat when—or if—he felt like it.

"How are your dad and mom holding up?" Natalie asked Scott when they were alone.

He shrugged. "As well as could be expected. Better—now that they're both leaning on the Lord. Of course, our family has a long way to go. But I think Mom's thinking of a Twelve-Step program, and Dad really believes it will be different this time." There was a slight pause. "I've . . . made up with Mom, Natalie. This is no time to turn my back on her."

"I'm so glad, Scott."

"It really meant a lot to her to know that your parents aren't blaming us."

"How is Zac taking all this?"

"He won't talk about it. He's really down. Wouldn't say a word all the way back. Says he's too ashamed to face anyone, even the family."

"We'll just have to keep praying."

"Thanks." He hesitated, then turned to smile at her—a heart-stopping smile. "That means a lot to me, Nat." Then he grew serious again. "But who knows what's going to happen now?"

Only God, Natalie thought. *Only God.*

It was late when Natalie and her parents left the lake house on their way home. The evening had gone well, with the Ainsworths promising to pray for the Lamberts and to stay in close touch. Lawrence and Helen would be staying with Zac at the lake until the hearing, with Dr. Lambert commuting to the hospital in Garden City each day. The rest of the family would join them on weekends.

"There's one more stop I need to make, Mom and Dad," Natalie said once they were in the car. "Could you drop me by the hospital for a few minutes?" She had no idea whether she would be allowed to see Katlyn, but she had to try.

Inside the sprawling building, Natalie took the elevator to the fourth floor and followed the arrows to the Medical Intensive Care Unit. The hallways appeared to be deserted. Only once did she pass a pink-smocked technician speaking with a doctor. The two were so engrossed in their discussion about a patient that they didn't notice when Natalie passed by, noiselessly, on the mauve carpet.

At the end of the corridor, she spotted a nurses' station, the command post for a glassed-in partition labeled MICU. A bank of computer screens constantly monitored heart and respiration, brain-wave activity, and other vital signs for the seriously ill patients confined in the restricted area.

Stepping up to the desk, Natalie took a deep breath. "I'd like to inquire about an accident victim— Katlyn Chander."

The plump nurse on duty seemed friendly enough, though distracted with her charts. Looking about,

Natalie saw that there was no one else in sight.

Finally, the nurse snapped a folder shut and looked up with a frown. "Sorry, ma'am. Visitors' hours are almost over. And on this floor, only family members are permitted."

Natalie was frantic. *I can't give up now.* "Look, I'm on my way out of town, so I *have* to see her tonight. This is really important to me."

The nurse gazed at her curiously. "You're the second person to say that—just last night, as a matter of fact. A young guy. Said they were . . . very close . . . that it was terribly important to him that she recover."

Scott. It had to be Scott. Natalie's heart sank to a new low. All those things he'd shared with her . . . the way he'd looked at her . . . none of it had meant anything. It was Katlyn he really cared about.

"Well, I suppose if I could let *him* in, I could make an exception for you, too," the nurse was saying, "especially since there is no family member around at the moment."

Natalie shook off her gloom. The most important thing right now was Katlyn's life. She could deal with losing Scott another time. "Uh . . . thanks a lot."

The nurse gave a nod. "Through that door. But only five minutes."

Natalie smiled her gratitude. Looking through the glass, she saw two figures in the walled-off room. One was obviously a male, judging from his close-cut beard; the other had to be Katlyn.

Natalie stepped into the room, standing a short distance from the hospital bed. If there had not been a chart with the name CHANDER in large letters, she would have thought she was in the wrong place. The broken person in the bed in no way resembled the bubbly girl Natalie remembered.

Not a square inch of her body—the part that was visible, at least—had been left unscathed. Her beautiful black hair had been shaved on one side, a bald spot spikey with black stitches. Needles and tubes protruded from nose, mouth, and arms. Both legs were encased in casts and suspended by pulleys. A respirator, gasping in a whooshing sound behind the bed, breathed in and out like some monster waiting to pounce.

Katlyn lay as still as death, the dark, laughing eyes swollen to slits. Bruises—like too much eyeshadow—smudged her face, puffy almost beyond recognition.

"Dear God," Natalie murmured in horror, "please don't let her die. . . ."

Natalie moved closer. What if she never saw Katlyn again? She had to make her understand. . . .

"Katlyn," she began in a small voice, "it's Natalie. I don't know if you can hear me, but I want you to know how sorry I am this happened." Natalie dropped her voice to a whisper. "But I'm even sorrier for the way I've felt about you.

"You see, it's Scott. I've never really liked a guy until he came along. After what happened during the tornado, we were getting to be really good friends . . . until you decided you'd like him to be more than friends.

"It's okay, though, Katlyn. Really. I'm going back to Garden City tonight, and Scott will stay on here with his family for a while. So you'll have lots of time to see each other. Just . . . please forgive me for caring more about myself and what I wanted than about you."

Natalie stared down at the black-and-white tile floor before lifting her head again. "There's just one more thing, Katlyn. I want you to have something." Natalie unclasped the little pin she was wearing on the collar of her bandana shirt. "When you get scared and need to feel God's love, hold on to this." She pinned the little dove on Katlyn's pillow. "He's one Friend who will never leave you."

Breathing one last prayer for the battered girl, Natalie left the room, took the elevator down to the lobby, and stepped out into the silent, starry night.

———

"I'm only sixteen, and my life's over!" Katlyn Chander cries bitterly. "I may never walk again!"

Katlyn's dad insists Zac Lambert will pay for what he's done. He should be thrown in prison for life!

Are Katlyn's and Zac's lives ruined? And how can Natalie Ainsworth be a friend to Katlyn, who wants to be more than a friend to Scott?

Discover the surprising answers in the next WHITE DOVE ROMANCE.